Thank !

All The Best

To You & Jill

Don

THE RING MASTER

A Murder Mystery

A Love Story

TOM SALVADOR

Bloomington, IN Milton Keynes, UK

authorHOUSE

AuthorHouse™
1663 Liberty Drive, Suite 200
Bloomington, IN 47403
www.authorhouse.com
Phone: 1-800-839-8640

AuthorHouse™ UK Ltd.
500 Avebury Boulevard
Central Milton Keynes, MK9 2BE
www.authorhouse.co.uk
Phone: 08001974150

First published by AuthorHouse 2/20/2006

ISBN: 1-4259-0810-1 (sc)

Printed in the United States of America
Bloomington, Indiana

This book is printed on acid-free paper.

Cover design by Cruzan Engineering

Books by Tom Salvador

The Midas Man
The Ring Master
The Host

Dedicated to *Love*
It is all that is needed
The rest of the rules you can throw away

❧ ACKNOWLEDGMENTS ❧

With warm thanks to Joseph Ostaseski, Jr., for his superb knowledge and for being true friend. And a huge thanks for his in-depth editing skills, my fellow Bronxite, Herb Shanker. Thanks also to my readers Lydia Russo and Brian Entin and to all of the other experts in their fields, notably, Cindy Baldwin, for their time and patience.

I would be remiss not to thank Bernadette for her love and her endurance shown while I was *living* in the book.

❧ PROLOGUE I ❧

Sunday April 4, 1982

Long Island, New York

"Hi Mrs. Labrador, this is Nick. Could I speak to Veronica, please?"

"Sure you can Nick, hold on."

"Veronica! VERONICA! It's Nick for you."

"I got it, Mom." Veronica called out.

She took the call in her room and closed her door.

"Hi. I thought you'd be over already."

"Yeah, me too, Roni, I'm a... kind a held up here with family... you know, things. I don't think I can make it to-night."

There was a pause.

"I'm disappointed. I really wanted to see you," she said.

There was another pause while he cleared his throat.

"I can't...but. Hey! I can get my father's car earlier tomorrow and come right over. We could go down to the beach."

"That really sounds good, Nick." Her voice reflected her let down. *He seems uneasy. Why?* Veronica's thoughts, even during church services, were only of Nick.

"Did you remember that tomorrow's ring day?" Veronica tried to not sound disappointed.

Nick hesitated as if preoccupied, "You know, I forgot what day it was." He paused again and then added, "We could exchange rings, right?"

"Yes, I would like that." *Again, that stressed tone in his voice.*

"Well then, I guess I'll see you tomorrow?"

"See you tomorrow, Nick."

She went to bed earlier than usual, wishing the night would pass quickly into tomorrow. It did, but not before Veronica gave in to her desires and slid to the edge of her bed, as was her way.

∾

Ring day energized the senior class with the first symbol of their graduation from high school. Most of the student body had placed their orders four months ago and now the rings were being delivered. In the hallway outside of the classroom in which the vendor set up shop, Veronica and Nick exchanged rings. After trying them on, he placed his ring into her jeans pocket. His familiarity pleased her. Classes changed and they went in separate directions.

One of Veronica's good friends, and the one who introduced her to Nick, was with her in the next class. Andrea was a cheerleader as was Veronica.

"Did you get your ring?" Andrea called out, as she came down the hallway toward Veronica.

"Yes, but you know who has it now?" She bubbled.

Andrea was wearing hers.

"Oh, you have the other style!" Veronica noticed.

Andrea pulled it off to show her and placed it into Veronica's hand.

Veronica's fingers instinctively closed on the ring to protect it.

The imagery came like frames of pictures in quick succession. Veronica's present time ceased to exist, as this new world blasted all else out of its way.

She dropped the ring, the sound of which brought her back, exhausted, to the school hallway.

"MY RING!" Andrea shouted in amazement as it bounced along the marble floor.

"You BITCH!" Veronica screamed.

"How could you? You're supposed to be my friend!"

Andrea was now amazed for another reason. "How did you......?"

Veronica had already turned and went running to the restroom knowing she was getting sick to her stomach.

The rest of the day Veronica spent going through the motions of being alive. She avoided Nick, walked home crying and went to her room to cry some more. Nicholas Vito, the best quarterback Armstrong High ever had and this year's Prom King, and Veronica Labrador, considered to be the prettiest girl in the school, captain of the cheerleaders and this year's Prom Queen, were not to have a future. At home, she turned her jeans upside down and spilled out Nick's ring.

It was scooped up with a piece of cardboard and placed into a box with other mementos from him to be mailed in the morning. Sobbing the whole time, she would not ask for help or involve her parents, who adored Nick.

She didn't want to see or speak to him. He tried to call and he tried to talk to her at school. She refused his calls and turned her back to him. She heard him say, "I'm sorry" as she walked away. He kept calling and trying. Finally, he gave up.

∽

Veronica's friends insulated her from the school gossip. By *circling the wagons* around her, the story was simple – he cheated and she found out. To her, it was a mystery which had something to do with Andrea's ring. This had never happened before and it would be *her* secret, not to be shared with anyone else. If she had spoken about it, she would have used her often repeated term, "spooky."

She looked radiant at the prom however, within her, the sun had ceased to shine. Veronica came alone and intended to leave after fulfilling her duties as Prom Queen. Nick did not have a date for the prom either.

The sparks reflecting off of the multi faceted revolving ball gave a surreal setting to an awkward dance. As they moved at arms length, Nick tried to draw her close, but Veronica stiffened up even more. She had not spoken to him since it happened.

"I'm so very sorry, Roni, he said pleading. "I love you. I never wanted to hurt you."

She looked up at him, and her eyes locked into his. Veronica, the high school cheerleader, was 5'6" while Nick was 6'1" and would never again throw another touchdown pass.

"Well, you did and you know that."

"I know," he said, lowering his head. "I didn't mean…"

Veronica interrupted. "And what we did wasn't good enough was it? We were both satisfied but, no, you had to have the real thing. Was that for your buddies to prove to them you're a real man? Was it some kind of a fucking jock initiation thing? You broke my heart, Nicky." Her tears started to flow.

"Well, you got the real thing from a fake of a friend. I hope you're fucking happy for the rest of your life. I'll never know."

The music ended and she walked coolly off of the dance floor, leaving him motionless within the fiery glitter.

❧ PROLOGUE II ❧

September, 2003

Cape Cod, Massachusetts

They arrived at the cottage before midnight, hungry for more than food. The take out doughnuts were devoured before going down to the river and diving off the end of the dock. Moonlight shimmered on their naked bodies as the splashing was foreplay to their craving. Still laughing, they toweled and dripped their way to the bed. It was a familiar routine.

They moved in unison to their own satisfaction. She enjoyed his roughness and wanted him to assert his dominance. Reaching her threshold, she arched her back. She didn't need him, never did. His hands switched position and her eyes grew wide with temporary glee. His pressure on her neck increased, turning her passion to fear. Her world grew black as she entered eternal darkness.

Before tonight they agreed it was best to remain apart. He couldn't let that be.

His wet suit and gear were in the closet. Tank, regulator, fins and light were all there. He attached the light to his wrist with a lanyard. A runaway lamp would create an unwanted light show.

The construction company, putting in the new bathroom, had left some heavy plastic supply bags and nylon cord. He placed her body into a double bag and onto a wheelbarrow. Before sealing her in with duct tape, he added a small boulder from the garden area for weight. He took her to the middle of the dock and together they entered the chilly water. It seemed colder to him then before.

She was secured in her plastic "mummy" wrapping as he descended. At the proper time, he pushed sideways toward the large boulders lining the river by the cottage. He knew of the "flat one" and placed her onto this boulder, sliding her into a miniature cave; her "sepulcher" among the rocks.

❧ CHAPTER ONE ❧

April 2005, New York City – The Present

"The Rathskeller" was its normal busy self with the in-crowd of after work professionals and pseudo-professionals. All makes and models of people and office dress obliterated the lack of serious decorations in this mid-town New York City gathering place. There were beer steins on shelves, German autobahn signs and German beer posters on the walls. The Bavarian theme permeated the place and the food. By 6:30 PM all that could be seen were heads. The large bar was front loaded and drew new patrons immediately into the party. There were small tables off to its left, but they were hardly ever used; mostly because they were out of the flow. The Rathskeller had an area in back for undisturbed dining which was one-third the size of the front. Food could also be ordered at the bar, which was the usual choice.

"Do you want another drink?"

"I don't think so, thank you, I have to catch the 9:42 back to Long Island," Veronica responded.

He shrugged his shoulders.

She wasn't even sure of his name. He had taken a seat next to her at the bar after she had eaten her dinner and after her former co-worker, Carol, had left. *He's just another guy that will disappear into the woodwork or, in this case, beer posters. No need to know his name.*

At forty years of age, Veronica was two pounds lighter then she was on graduation day from Armstrong High. Equally unchanged was her straight cut golden brown hair with a hint of red, flowing just beyond her shoulders. She kept her body taut by jogging, playing tennis and doing her pilates, but it was her face that captivated most men. Veronica's sparkling crystal blue eyes contrasting with her perennial tan put the insecure on weak knees. Her personal life since high school consisted of two serious relationships and numerous dates, none lately. She had yet to find love. Veronica defined it as, *that emotional tugging at her heart...that profound tearing away of all pretenses and barriers to her soul.* She would not accept anything less.

Now that she had left the CPA firm of Herzog & Herzog and taken a job with one of their clients, her dress code was more to her liking. Stodginess was out and chic was in. Her new job was with a business that serviced the entertainment industry and they had hired her as assistant controller. She was in charge of all tax matters. Her office friends were still at the CPA firm, Carol being one of them.

She paid her tab, said goodbye to the bartender, Ralph, and thanked whoever his name was again for the offer of a drink and was out the door into the cool of the night. The

Long Island Rail Road Station was only two blocks away and she was a quick walker. *Only a few more days of this hustle and this tough commute will be over,* she thought. Veronica had purchased a co-op on East 74th Street.

She crossed 34th street and went down the escalator into the world below the city. The electronic arrival and departure board told her that her train would be leaving from track fourteen. It was already boarding when she went down another set of stairs to the platform. Veronica walked down the aisle between seats until she found one that was facing forward. She didn't like to ride backwards and neither did a majority of the other passengers. She put her attaché case beside her, crossed her legs and tried not to think of anything. A man diagonally across from her glanced at her legs then looked away. She ignored him and didn't change her position. Veronica dozed off for a period and did not wake at the stop before hers, Hicksville, but was wide awake by the time the train rolled into the next station, Syosset. She had sold her house on Long Island and was living with her good friend, Geraldine McCabe, while her co-op in the city was being painted and re-decorated. Veronica had known her since high school. Even at this late hour there were enough passengers disembarking as to make it safe. The car she was using was a rental and was waiting in the parking lot.

She unlocked the door of the split level house and found the lights on. "Gerry? GERRY? GERALDINE!" No answer. Gerry hated the name Geraldine. Veronica checked the house. There was no one home. *Two more weeks and maybe there'll be a little more excitement in my life.*

She was in the process of re-reading "The Iliad." Hector was her favorite character, not the gilded Achilles. Two chapters later, she went off to bed.

In the morning, the routine started again. They each made their own cereal breakfast.

"Good morning! You got in late," Veronica added.

"How would you know Roni, you were busy cutting down a whole forest when I got home."

"I don't snore. Anyway, did you see him again?"

"Yeah, out at the Stratford where everyone leaves at 3AM."

"He's married Gerry, it's not going to lead to anything."

Gerry paused with her spoon just coming out of the bowl. Her face beginning to match the color of her shag cut auburn hair.

"You said you would never lecture me. And you DO snore! And what's so exciting about your life?"

"I…", Veronica hesitated, "I was wrong. I'm sorry Gerry."

"I'm sorry too, I shouldn't have snapped. It's just that you have the "stuff" to pick and choose and I think that's great. For now, I enjoy being with John, that's his name, it's not *him*." Gerry smiled at her own remark and then they hugged.

Veronica stepped back and said, "Okay, I got it. I won't go there again, but don't sell yourself short either. Remember you were every guy's fantasy; a cheerleader. He makes you feel good? That's all that matters."

"He's got the goods," Gerry replied.

They laughed going out the door to their cars and left in separate directions.

❦ CHAPTER TWO ❦

From 34th Street, where Penn Station commingled with the Long Island Rail Road Station, Veronica could walk to her office if she chose. It was sixteen city blocks to 50th. If the air was crisp she would "walk it up," but most of the time she took the subway. She had a nice corner office, 19 floors above Broadway. By looking down to the street, she could check the weather and check the styles. Veronica preferred the shorter length skirts, not mini's, but not suffragette lengths either. Her choice of style accented her still cheerleader body.

On Friday, Veronica had lunch with Gerry McCabe who had come into the city on company business. After eating in the luncheonette on the ground floor of Veronica's office building, they took the E train to Lexington and 68th and from there they *hoofed it* to Veronica's new co-op apartment on the East Side at 74th Street and Lexington Avenue.

"Do you like all this walking? You must!" Gerry answered her own question. "And look at all of the bars, lounges or whatever you want to call them!"

"I'm just noticing them for the first time myself," said Veronica.

"I have a feeling this move is going to be more than just a different address for you, Roni. I really do."

"How do you stay so positive? You're like my personal court jester. Actually, you're more like the sister I never had. I hope you're right. I'm making this move to bring my job and my home closer. Who knows, maybe my social life will improve too?" My "stuff," as you say, didn't get me a controller's job like some guys in my office did. When I went looking, the only offer that I received was for assistant controller. I took it because I liked the company; it's solid, and I got to know the management from doing the audits there. Sometimes I feel this "stuff" is a detriment."

Gerry took all of this in without comment.

"Here we are! Veronica pointed to the building.

"Ooo, a doorman!" Gerry exclaimed.

"Hi Charles, I'm Veronica, remember me? I'll be moving in soon."

He nodded his greeting and then said hello to Gerry.

As they walked through the vestibule, Gerry turned around, "Nice butt."

"You're incorrigible." Veronica responded.

It was only four flights up and Veronica led the way to the stairwell.

"You sure are a glutton for this walking."

The painters were almost finished. Veronica on seeing this said, "Maybe I'll get my stuff out of storage on Monday and begin the transition from Long Island to New York."

"Sounds like a plan." As soon as she said it, Gerry remembered that overused phrases bothered Veronica. "Sorry," she added.

"Veronica laughed. You make me laugh, something I should do more often. How about next Friday, when I'm all moved in, .we hit the hot spots around here?"

"Okay, but we don't have to decide anything now, remember we *are* living together."

Veronica thought to herself, as to what a good friend Gerry has been, for so many years.

They walked back to the station at 68th Street and took the train back to 50th Street. Gerry stayed on to 34th Street and the Long Island Rail Road.

The rest of the day involved meetings with her staff, as to the collection of data especially from their subsidiary companies. And then a meeting with the upper management, as to the effect of the new tax laws on their industry and company.

By the end of the day, Veronica was all talked out.

∾

The weekend was uneventful with Veronica declining an offer from Gerry to a blind double date with one of her friend's friend. Veronica could never remember his name because she didn't want to know it. She didn't even ask if the one who would have been her date was married. Since she was declining, there wasn't any need to know, and it might get Gerry upset.

The painters were gone on Monday and Veronica was moved in by Wednesday. She worked fast and the apartment was respectable by Friday.

Gerry came with her overnight bag.

"Well, this is a switch, you staying at my house."

"I enjoyed having your company for, what was it, three and a half weeks?"

"Thanks for putting up with me, Gerry. Now get yourself comfortable, get freshened up and let's go hit those local bars. I'll whip us up a couple of microwave dinners."

They left the apartment, Veronica in a little black dress, Gerry in a white man tailored silk blouse, short green skirt and matching green jacket. "Just in case they can't see that I'm Irish; whoever and wherever "they" are."

The doorman was the same as last Friday. He said his goodnights to them and then turned to walk back toward the vestibule. Gerry also turned.

"Stop it!" Veronica giddily blurted out.

Down the block and around the corner they came to "The 546" and went in. It was neither dark nor bright. It had just the right light so as to not be surprised by a stranger showing up for the first date. The layout looked to be the same as The Rathskeller. They found two stools mid-way down the bar and ordered drinks. Gerry excused herself while Veronica waited for their drinks.

Something got into Veronica's left eye. *Where's Gerry when I need her and why couldn't she use the bathroom at my place?* Veronica took out a little mirror, but couldn't see anything. Now her other eye was becoming strained.

It was a deep voice. "I could help you."

With her good eye, Veronica noticed that a man had slid over to Gerry's stool. Her left eye was bothering Veronica so badly that it was making her right eye tear. She couldn't make out his features. His face was a wet blur. Veronica didn't remember saying yes, but it was out as soon as his gentle hands touched her eyelids.

❦ Chapter Three ❦

"Are you a doctor or something?"

"Let's just say that I'm someone and I go around putting things in attractive women's eyes so that I can take it or them out. My name is Bill Vito, and?"

"My name is …Vito?

"Vito? You have my last name?"

"No, no it's definitely not Vito."

"All right, before we lapse into "Abbot and Costello," take a deep breath, think about your name and then say it."

"It's Veronica Labrador."

"I knew you could do it. That's a pretty name and it fits. Now, what was all that Vito business?"

"My old boyfriend's name, from high school, was Vito." This was said on the verge of laughter.

"It was his first name?" Bill Vito had this incredulous look on his face causing Veronica to go from the big smile to giggles to uncontrollable laughter. Tears were rolling down her cheeks; this time not from an errant eyelash.

"His name was Nick Vito" she said through her laughing tears. *The last time his name was uttered her tears were bitter.*

"You can rest easy. There aren't any Nicks in my family."

"And who has been and still is sitting on my stool?" Gerry said in a low deep voice. She added in her normal voice, "Did you tickle her? I haven't seen her like this since, (*she thought high school but did not say it*) …maybe I've never seen her like this."

"I brought my own porridge Miss Wolf I didn't drink yours. I'll move,"

"No… no please stay. I'll take your seat. You can sit between us." She held out her hand, "I'm Gerry McCabe."

"Glad to meet you, "I'm Bill Vito."

"Vito?" Gerry questioned.

"I got it, you're a tag team." He said it pointing to Gerry and wearing a big smile.

"He's no relation to the Vito we knew." Veronica jumped in.

"Oh, all right then. Were you crying? I only went to the restroom and I feel like I've been gone a year. Could you bring my life up to date for the last five minutes?"

"While you were gone something flew in my eye and Bill took it out. That's it. It took much longer to get past the Vito business. But we have."

She nodded at Bill who nodded back.

Veronica paused to observe the physical Bill Vito for the first time. He looked to be about six feet tall, regular build, not overly handsome. He had a great smile and a better personality. *He's not dull, so he's probably not an accountant; which I guess is an unfair judgment.*

Bill pushed his stool away from the bar to include Gerry in the conversation. Veronica liked that. It turned out that he was an accountant after all, but was now working in business sales. He didn't talk about himself but rather made both Veronica and Gerry feel important. Veronica's heart ached for moments like this.

She believed this emotional feeling was coming from bringing Nick's name up in public for the first time in over twenty years. As the evening wore on, it became apparent that this was not the case. It was Bill Vito. He seemed honest, attentive and he cured her eye problem. He also made her laugh and that put him to the head of the class; empty as it were.

Their eyelids couldn't keep up with the evening and finally won over. They exchanged telephone numbers and Bill made a promise to call them. It was addressed to both Veronica and Gerry, but Gerry knew it was Veronica that he would call. Veronica declined his offer to walk them back to her apartment. She didn't know where this would go and wanted to reveal her personal life on her own terms. Veronica told him that she and Gerry would be too much for any attacker. He laughingly agreed.

As they walked back to the apartment, the evening was critiqued. Nice guy, nice personality, nice, nice, nice.

"I haven't seen you this happy, maybe since high school, Roni."

"You said that. Have I been that morbid? And do I need a guy that badly?"

"Okay, I'm sorry. I know I'm pushing. It's just that tonight I saw you genuinely happy. I don't know about you, but it did make *me* feel good."

"Do you ever hear about Jim?" Gerry said, changing the subject to Veronica's last serious relationship.

"Yes, and only recently. I heard he's married with two children. He really did love me and I broke his heart. And, as much as it hurt me to do the right thing for the both of us, I'm sure it didn't compare to what he felt. I know that."

Gerry knew she was referring to Nick. Maybe Nick was never far from Veronica's thoughts? Once they split, Gerry never heard her mention him again.

"I said his name tonight. After all of this time, isn't that weird?"

Gerry didn't think so, but did not disagree.

Veronica went on. "Talk about coincidence, I saw Nick's name in the paper last week. It seems he was instrumental in solving an old case."

Nicholas Vito's name was often in the paper and he was one of the NYPD's rising stars in homicide investigation.

"Maybe I'm stepping over the line, especially since I told you not to do it to me, but do you still have feelings for Nick? If it's going to upset you, forget I even said anything."

"You're my oldest and best friend who never prodded me about details. To answer your question, I don't think about him at all. His name tonight was a *word* and not a person. And to answer your next question, before you ask it, yes, I would give Bill a chance, if he calls."

"Oh, he'll call all right!"

Veronica rolled her eyes. "Goodnight Gracie."

"Goodnight Roni."

Veronica left Gerry in the living room with the sofa bed and fresh linens. She closed the door to her bedroom and, turning her head, looked behind into a full length mirror.

"Gerry's right," she laughed.

They ate breakfast in and had lunch out in one of the better restaurants.

"Everything here is around the corner," Gerry remarked.

"Not everything, Gerry. We aren't. I enjoyed being your guest so, don't be a stranger in my home."

"I had a good time Roni and I know that I can do better than you know who. Maybe I'll meet someone like Bill?"

"If you want him, you can have him."

"Thanks, but I'd probably go for the doorman first."

After lunch, they walked together to the train station. Gerry went down the stairs into the subway, turned and waved back.

∾

He didn't call that evening but he did call the next day, Sunday. Veronica wasn't home and the message was taken by the answering machine. She didn't return the call.

∾

Mondays in accounting never seemed to disappoint Veronica. Things went wrong and previously completed tasks were found to have errors. Veronica was building a reputation of being as honest with her work as she was loyal to her staff. All mistakes she corrected without comment. Missteps never went beyond her office and, if they did, she would accept responsibility. Her bosses appreciated this approach. Sick calls were down and productivity was up. She was secure within herself and didn't need anyone to look bad for her to look good.

❧ CHAPTER FOUR ❧

In comparison to Monday, the rest of the week was uneventful. On Friday, Veronica left work early to join Carol for a sandwich and a drink. She was going to bring Veronica up to date with her former job's office politics.

Veronica stepped through the entrance of The Rathskeller and stood looking over a sea of heads. She spotted Carol, who had captured two stools at the bar. Veronica made her way through the crowd, excusing herself as she went along. She didn't have much trouble as the male patrons melted a path toward Carol. Veronica wasn't taken up with their attention and it sometimes put her ill at ease.

She sat in the empty stool and turned to her left to greet Carol. This is when she saw Bill. He looked to be in a serious conversation with a man who looked familiar. She remembered, it was Ken somebody, from one her previous firm's clients; a small graphic design company. His name is Kenneth. Her intuition told her, *don't go over.* She didn't, and turned her attention back to Carol and getting a drink.

"I'll take a scotch sour on the rocks, please. Thank you."

"Do you come here often?"

She didn't hear him come upon her. All of her attention was focused on the bartender and ordering a drink.

"And just how many times have you used, that, corny line?" She said without turning.

"It's a first. I usually come armed with a handful of dust and throw it in their eyes."

Veronica turned in her stool toward the voice. She was stirring her drink and smiling.

"You got here fast. I saw you over there, she pointed. You were speaking with someone who I think my former firm did business with. It looked pretty serious."

Bill seemed taken aback.

"I believe his name is Ken or maybe Kenneth?" she continued.

"That's right. Ken Small is an old friend of mine. We were talking about how things have changed between us. At one time, he and his wife and I all worked together in the same office. I guess nothing ever stays the same. His wife, who is now teaching high school on the Island, has filed for divorce."

Veronica acknowledged Bill by shaking her head, but didn't add to the conversation.

"So are you bar hopping?" Bill asked.

"Not really. I stopped off here a lot when I was commuting to Long Island. I love their brisket sandwich." She interrupted herself. "Oh, I'm being rude. I want you to meet my friend, Carol. She worked with me in my last job."

Small conversation followed until Carol excused herself to catch a train back to Long Island. "You remember how that is," she said to Veronica.

An awkward silence followed Carol's departure, which was broken by Bill.

"I called you," he said.

"I know, I just haven't had the time get back to anyone. You know with the new apartment and stuff."

"I'm not pressuring you, but you did have time to come here. I don't want to force you to do anything you don't want, Veronica; I just would like to know if I'm wasting both our times by trying to see you."

She was going to say something like she shouldn't have to account for her time, but didn't. He was right. If she didn't feel right about it, then it was over before it started. If not, then …..

"All right, I do want to see you. *There I said it.* And please accept this as a returned phone call so we can move forward, beyond "do you come here often." So here is my first question in our new beginning, have you ever been married?"

"Yes I have been married, but I'm not married now. No children. Is there anything else? I'm an open book. What about you?"

"I was engaged once, after college." She shrugged her shoulders. "There's nothing else of interest to add." She wanted to ask how long was he married and when was, what she assumed was, the divorce, but decided to leave that for another time.

They had another round of drinks and noted the crowd beginning to thin out. Their conversation outlasted their common interests and they simultaneously came off of their stools.

"I don't even know where you live?" Veronica questioned.

"I have a home in Queens. I use the subway to get there."

The air was brisk. He buttoned up his sport jacket and Veronica was glad she had her leather jacket to go along with her jeans and boots. As they walked down the street toward her subway entrance, his hand joined her willing hand and their fingers entwined. At the entrance to her station, they kissed lightly.

"I'll call you," he said.

"I'll call you back," she answered.

❧ CHAPTER FIVE ❧

He called the next day. Veronica declined dinner for that night but they made a date for the following Saturday. The week was quiet except for one visitor. Kenneth Small had contracted some business with her company and stopped in to say hello.

"When I was the auditor for your last firm I don't remember saying two words to you, or maybe it was two words." Veronica said as she extended her hand. Kenneth Small's forearm was muscular, which tied into his sturdy build. *He was pleasant, but not as carefree as Bill.*

"Yeah, Billy and I go back a long way. We did a lot of things together."

He looked up and seemed to be reminiscing.

"I didn't see you at *The* Rathskeller the other night, but when Bill described you I knew right away," he said.

"Bill, or Billy as you call him, spoke of you in a good way." *Veronica was going to say he spoke of you highly, except he didn't say anything about him other then that he was getting a divorce.* She was just making small talk. *She laughed to herself over her play on words.* He told her that he had a new job and she asked him how his new business was going. He explained the accounting system which he thought would be of interest to Veronica; it wasn't. There were more pleasantries exchanged and they shook hands again. *She came to the same conclusion as before, pleasant but not happy. Then again, with the divorce who would be?*

∞

Bill drove into the city and parked at a nearby garage. The doorman let him in.

Veronica received the "call up' from the doorman and was waiting in her doorway.

"Very nice, this is very nice. And it's decorated with taste. I like it!"

"Thanks, Bill and please excuse the boxes, I'm still unpacking. I have decorations for each holiday. I found Halloween and Thanksgiving, but I'm not sure if I know where all the Christmas decorations are. I think I have a couple of missing angels."

"I know one angel that's not missing."

Veronica didn't respond to his remark.

"So where are we going, do we need a taxi?" Veronica asked.

"No, we're going right around the corner."

"Now you sound like my good friend Gerry."

Bill's facial expression was a question.

"I'll explain at dinner."

∞

D'Arco's Restaurant was a *real* Italian restaurant according to Veronica. The menu was in Italian without English subtitles. She searched for something familiar and couldn't make a selection. The menu was the first surprise, the second surprise was that Bill spoke Italian. Her problem was solved.

Once the waiter, Anthony, learned that Bill could understand Italian he didn't bother to speak English again. She told Bill what she wanted and he did the ordering.

"So how is it that you can speak Italian?"

"Well, let's see…although my parents didn't carry the language over to my sister and me, I knew that my grandparents liked the fact that I could say some words in Italian. I loved my grandparents, so, to make them happier, I learned to speak their language."

Anthony brought their drinks; a strawberry daiquiri for her and a Manhattan straight-up for him.

"How long were you married?" she blurted out.

He hesitated then said, "It's a painful subject for me, but I don't blame you for asking. I certainly would."

"I'm an accountant remember. I'm a glutton for details," she said, hoping to lighten the conversation or at least his response.

Bill took a deep breath. He put his hand under his chin and then removed it.

"It seems…let me see. How do I say this?" He put his hand back under his chin.

"Look Bill, I don't want to ruin a great evening. God knows I haven't seen many lately. Let's change the subject. What do you think of the…"

"No," Bill interrupted. "You asked a reasonable question and it deserves an answer. I was having trouble with my marriage. I can't fault either one of us. Two years ago my wife disappeared from the home we had on Long Island. I couldn't stand the memories, so I moved to Queens last year. Clarice disappeared without a trace and, as her husband, I became the number one source of information and the number one suspect. There wasn't any evidence of foul play, I didn't have a girlfriend, and I had nothing to gain, so they lightened up on me. I hope she's safe, but I don't think so. She's a decent person who I think met up with someone who took advantage of her. We just fell out of love and probably would have gotten a divorce anyway.

He paused again.

"I bet you didn't expect this kind of an answer to your rather average question."

It was Veronica's turn to reflect. She reached across the table and placed her hand on top of his.

"Our lives are sometimes governed by events we can't control. We end up having to explain away those we neither initiated nor wanted. So we'll go on from here and hope we have some fun."

"You're Okay, Veronica. How have you lasted out there in the single world so long? Don't answer that! Lucky for me!"

A second round of drinks was served along with the salad and they both opted for water with a twist of lime when Anthony returned again with the main course. Veronica couldn't pronounce her entrée and, after a couple of tries, she gave up. She will tell Gerry that she had pasta and leave it at that.

They both refused the dessert menu and declined the after dinner drink. When Anthony brought the bill, he was

greeted with: *"Cosa ne penzi della mia ragazza?"* Anthony
returned with: *"E molto bella e' bellissima!"*

The way Anthony looked at her while he was answering
Bill, Veronica knew what was said pertained to her.

"Could you please tell me what you just said to him?"
Veronica questioned.

"I said, what do you think of my date, isn't she beautiful? And, he said, she is beyond beautiful. Of course this is
loosely translated."

Veronica was blushing.

"You really don't know do you? You turned the head of
every guy in this place. They all want to be sitting in my
chair."

"You're exaggerating, Bill, but tell me how do *you* feel?"

"I'll tell you how I feel, I'm a guy and I'm in this place.
The best part is that we're sitting at the same table. I'm the
lucky one."

"You said that before. Maybe we're both lucky."

∾

They walked holding hands to the parking garage and
Bill drove her home from there. At the front of her building,
Veronica still had not given any indication of inviting him
in. She had been mulling this over from the time he paid
their bill.

"Would you like to come up and see my place and have
a coffee for the road?"

*It was an impulsive move for Veronica to take and she
hoped that he would not take it that way. She had still not
made up her mind to ask him when she went and asked him
anyway.*

"That sounds good, but now we must find a space for this car." They drove around for over fifteen minutes before they found someone leaving their spot; about a block and a half away. By this time, Veronica was having second thoughts.

The doorman was not Gerry's and was someone who Veronica had not seen before. They went through the vestibule and walked up to her apartment.

"You keep in shape this way?" Bill said from behind.

"I try to." She felt vulnerable and wondered what he was looking at that was staying in shape.

Veronica made coffee while Bill walked around the living room looking at the decorations and pictures. All at once he was standing behind her and placed his hands on her hips. As they began to slide down she reached behind and placed both of her hands on his, halting their movement. Bill took his hands from under hers and placed them on her shoulders and turned her around toward him.

"I don't need more than coffee tonight and I don't need anything more at this point then a trusting relationship. You have what the world can see and you have an inner beauty of which you have allowed me to glimpse at. If you think that I want to get you into that bedroom over there, you had better believe it.

Who wouldn't? When that time comes, I plan to be first in line."

Veronica put her arms around his neck and kissed him, knowing that she would let him take it further. His hungry kiss drove her back and this time she let his hands rove. By backing up she led the way into the room and onto her bed.

Bill removed all but his boxer shorts while Veronica slipped under the sheets and removed what was left. He took a condom from its wrapper, which both surprised her and placed her at ease. She was taken aback again as he stood up and returned to the doorway and, instead of using the dimmer switch, he completely shut off the lights.

Bill's gentle touch was carried over from how he met her. He was finished before penetration, leaving Veronica with conflicting feelings of disappointment for him and a surprise relief for her. She had tried to help him, but he moved his hand to block the way.

"Are you all right?" he asked.

"It doesn't take much," she lied. *How could he not know? Unless? But... that's Gerry's department.*

When Bill rose out of her bed to use the bathroom, Veronica purposefully looked at him through the dim light. Bill had negotiated the dark bedroom; however, the bathroom light produced a revealing silhouette.

It doesn't matter to me she thought; for Gerry it's another matter. The thought of Gerry's opinion amused her. *Too bad she would never find out.*

Bill stayed for a cup of coffee and then kissed her at the door. "I'll call you tomorrow."

"I'll take the call," she smiled.

🎇 CHAPTER SIX 🎇

Veronica walked the city on Sunday and reflected both on her actions and Bill's character. She couldn't determine at what point spontaneity took over leading them to her bedroom. His performance in bed didn't bother her as much as her own mixed feelings afterwards.

Gerry's was the first call in on Monday morning.

"Well, how did it go?" she bubbled into the phone.

"Good…good really good. It went well."

"You got laid, didn't you?"

"Gerry please, it was just a date."

"Great! I knew it…I won't ask anymore questions."

"Good."

"So tell me…"

"GERALDINE, you said no questions."

"Okay, I'll stop. I'll bring it up at another time when it's not so new."

Gerry laughed into her end of the phone while Veronica gave a less than enthusiastic response.

"Bill has a friend, Ken, whom he would like you to meet. I told him all about you and he still wants you to meet his friend."

"Ha, Ha," came from Gerry.

Veronica continued, "I happened to have already met him. He worked at a place where, on my last job, we were their outside accounting firm. When he found out that I was Bill's friend, he stopped by my office. He was here on some kind of promotion for his firm and made a personal visit to my office. He seems nice enough even though he's going through the stress of a divorce."

"Maybe this is a forward step for me since my current gig will never get a divorce. I'll go for it. Set it up."

∽

Veronica and Bill met for lunch twice during the week and planned the double date for the coming Saturday.

"I met Gerry and she is a lot of fun. What do you think of her and Ken?" He said.

"It might work. You never know how good the chemistry between Gerry and Ken could be. What if we went back to "D'Arco's" for dinner? You can get to use your impressive Italian again."

"Is that what attracted you? And I though it was my animal magnetism."

"It was neither. You come across as very innocent and that'll get me every time. Innocent and nice; those are good qualities." *I still don't have those heart wrenching, heart panging feelings. Maybe I never will and maybe it's a myth.*

❦ Chapter Seven ❦

Gerry came in to New York City on Friday night and stayed over at Veronica's for Saturday "date night" at D'Arco's Ristorante. Friday, however, was girl's night. They had TV dinners at the condo and were out for drinks and some laughs.

"I was disappointed in your doorman tonight."

"Well, he's not 24/7. He has to have time to keep that butt you like in shape. You have all day tomorrow to get lucky." Surprisingly, Gerry seemed happy about that.

Gerry was amused as once again they went around the corner from Veronica's condo to a new place, Frank's Bistro and Lounge. The interior looked the same as other places.

"The people are starting to look the same too." Gerry mentioned.

"Have a drink and they'll begin to change, usually for the better."

"So how are ye doin?"

He had taken the stool next to Veronica and was talking to the back of her head. She looked at Gerry who rolled her eyes.

"How do you even know what I look like?" Veronica still had not turned around.

"Oh, I saw ye when ye came in. A real doll! Good pins, too."

"Pins?"

"Yeah, pins, legs."

Gerry came down from her stool.

"Look mac, that's it. You're very nice, but we're expecting someone to be here very shortly and he wouldn't be happy if we were speaking to another guy."

He stepped toward Gerry, who didn't budge.

"You stay outa this sister."

"Girls, is this gentleman bothering you?" He had come from behind them.

Without waiting for an answer, he stepped in front of Gerry and stood face to face with the intruder.

"Now we can do this in a nice way or we can do this down and dirty. I really don't care which way we go. It's your call, chief."

"Ahh you're probably a couple a dykes anyway. A couple of lesbos. Yeah lesbos, that's it." He backed away and melted into the crowd.

"What rock did he crawl out from under?" said Veronica. She added, "And, Gerry, I would like to introduce you to your date for tomorrow, Kenneth Small."

"Ken, you can call me Ken. How are you Gerry?"

Gerry turned to Veronica.

"I like him Roni, good choice."

"I didn't choose him; he came with Bill's package." As soon as she said it, Veronica wanted to take it back. Gerry, however, was on good behavior and let it alone. They had one more drink, which Ken bought. He told them that he had worked late and had come here with one of the partners from his firm and would be returning to The Bronx. As soon as the divorce was settled, he would have money from the house to get something in Manhattan. They walked Ken to his subway entrance.

He shook Veronica's hand while Gerry gave him a kiss on the cheek.

"Thank you for saving us, Gerry said.

"Aw shucks maam, it tweren't nuth'n," he said as he shuffled his feet. He then stopped his act and said, "I'll see you girls tomorrow. I'm looking forward to it."

The night was clear and brisk. Veronica set the pace.

"Thanks for letting "package" go. I didn't think you would, but then I never really know with you. You must have really liked him?"

"I did Roni, and he was much better than the description you gave."

"I have to say you're right. He was much better than I originally thought."

They went to bed with the idea that they would have a good breakfast out with just a snack before dinner with the boys.

ॐ

Bill Vito had driven to The Bronx and picked up Ken Small. After putting Bill's car in the nearby parking garage, they walked to Veronica's apartment.

"Nice to see you again," Gerry said to the both of them.

Bill and Veronica kissed.

The doorman was Gerry's favorite. This time she didn't give him any notice.

At D'Arco's Ristorante, they asked for Dominic who gave them all a greeting but reserved the biggest smile for Veronica.

Bill leaned close to Veronica and spoke into her ear, "I think he likes you." He then ordered a bottle of cabernet for the table and proceeded to explain the menu to Veronica and Gerry. Ken, to Veronica's amazement, could handle the Italian, though not as well as Bill.

"Now how is it that you, too, have this as your second language?" asked Veronica.

"You see Bill had this grandmother who loved to hear Bill speak Italian and since I was at his house almost every day, I learned to speak a limited version."

"You and Bill know each other since you were kids?" Veronica spoke.

"Yeah, we went to grammar school, high school and even went to the same college. If this were Utah, we might have married the same girl." Ken laughed and continued, "Every year we went for about three weeks to Cape Cod to Bill's uncle's place. It was great and we felt rich."

"I got an idea," Bill said. "Why don't we take some time off and head up to the Cape for some R and R. My Uncle Joe now lives in Florida and I go up every so often to make sure everything is intact. Does either one of you scuba dive?"

"We both do," said Veronica.

"Great then, before we leave here tonight, we'll pick a date," said Bill. "The key is still kept in the top of the lamp post near the front door," he added while looking at Ken.

"I haven't been there in a while, but that's where it was my last time," said Ken.

❧ CHAPTER EIGHT ❧

Gerry didn't consummate her weekday rendezvous; instead, on Friday night, she drove into The Bronx to see Ken. He was renting an apartment off Boston Post Road until the divorce was settled.

"Hi Gerry, it's not that great, huh? But, it's for the time being, my only castle," said Ken as he led her into the foyer.

She had to admit from the outside it didn't look that good. It was a three story building that was in need of a good resurfacing. She didn't share that with him. The inside was another story.

"Hey, this is great for a bachelor. It's very neat and tidy." She turned around from viewing the apartment and their eyes met. He kissed her and she hungrily kissed him back. He reached behind her and closed the door. All the foreplay had occurred during the week with their telephone conversations. They had spoken a few times in the beginning and many times at the end of the week. By Friday, Gerry was out of control.

Ken's body was strong from a lifetime of lifting weights. He looked good to Gerry and she wanted him to have the same feeling. Her jeans and white blouse accented her figure and the white sneakers finished off her casual look. She was not sleek, like Veronica, but would not be overlooked in a swimsuit contest.

It was over too fast for her. As they lay side by side, she took hold of his hand. Before she could guide it down her stomach, he was ready to go again. This time he took longer and it was enough time for her.

Their bodies glistened with sweat as again they lay next to each other.

"Do you work out?" Ken said, as he moved his hand over her flat stomach.

"You mean besides what we just did? Yes, I do pilates and I have a treadmill."

"You *are* funny Gerry and you have a great body." Personality and body, that's a winning combination," Ken stood up and began to get dressed. She took his cue and did the same.

"Am I overdoing it by taking you to an Italian restaurant? They have some great ones here in The Bronx."

"I don't have any problem with that. I love Italian food."

He drove through the bumpy streets and not so good looking neighborhoods. One more turn and two blocks later the complexion of the scenery had changed. Affluent had replaced worn and in the middle of it all was this upscale restaurant, "Vincent's." After dinner, Gerry didn't look to go back to his apartment and, Ken noticing that, didn't further pursue her.

"I'm very tired Ken. I had a good time with you and *everything* and I want to do it *all* again." She gave him a reassuring kiss and he held her tightly. As she crossed the Throgs

Neck Bridge, she hoped that it would continue as she said. She didn't want to go back to her dead end affair.

On Sunday, Gerry tried to call Veronica, but could not get through.

∾

Veronica didn't want to spend every weekend with Bill, and was glad when he said he would be away on business this coming Wednesday through Sunday. Gerry called Veronica at her office on Monday and said she would take her up on her invitation to stay with her Friday night. Saturday night, Gerry said that she would be seeing Ken.

∾

"Wow! You got this place looking good, Roni. It does look like it belongs with a doorman out front."

"I thought you didn't need the doorman anymore?"

"I don't, besides, Ken has a better butt."

"Please don't tell me anything further. I don't want to know and I shouldn't know," said Veronica with a smirk.

"That's the good ear talking. Which is the bad ear that wants to hear all the good stuff?" Gerry mischievously answered.

"You can always make me laugh, Gerry. There *is* something that I would like to ask you."

"Now you're talking."

"No I'm not. It's just this one thing and it's not about sex."

"It just so happens I have something to speak to you about and it's something to do with sex," Gerry countered.

"Why am I not surprised?" Veronica giggled.

They decided to forego the TV dinners and eat at "The 546." It was early, but the front was filling up fast. There were tables in the back which was better than eating at the bar and risk having some one's elbow in your food.

"So you tell me first and then I'll show you mine," said Gerry.

Veronica smiled and shook her head, "I know you're going to be all over my case with this but I just don't think I have the right feelings toward Bill."

"You're right, I think you're crazy. What's there not to like about Bill, and maybe even love? Give love a chance. Give love a chance. Give Bill a chance."

She chanted.

Veronica was laughing. "You had me going there for a moment and then the real Gerry showed up."

"I really do mean it, Roni; he seems like such a nice guy. You don't want to tell me any of the sordid details, so I can't comment on that. I would like to. But from what I can see, he seems genuine."

"So you think I'm wrong?"

"This is a switch, you asking me. I like him. I've gotten to know Ken well and he's more of my type. A little rough around the edges, but, I believe, honest. Bill is more your type. We seemed to have matched out pretty good."

"Gerry, listen, maybe I'm missing something, maybe I'm looking for something that will never be there and maybe you're right and I'm absolutely wrong. But if I don't feel that yearning, if I can just let him ride off into the sunset without missing him, is this right?"

"He went away for a couple of days, Roni. He probably left in the morning before any sunrise let alone a sunset. And I doubt very much that he went off on a horse."

"Is there a time when you're not "on" Gerry?" But I have to say, you do make sense in between all of the joking around. You're probably right, I'll give it more time to like him better. *She purposely did not say love.* So what is it you have to tell me? And keep in mind that I never advanced beyond Sex 101."

"Okay, lets see, since you don't want to hear any of the blow by blow descriptions, no pun intended, this is what Ken said to me while we were in his refractory period. Do you want to know that he had two of these before we went to dinner?"

"No," said Veronica smiling.

"Anyway, it was the second one and it was the last one because we had to go to dinner."

"Please spare me," said Veronica, grinning.

"He said a girlfriend of his liked to experience pain with her sex and so did his wife. He asked me if this was a current trend. I told him, not with me it isn't. I proceeded to tell him all the things I did do, such as ..."

"Stop! Please, no details. Besides, you told me on other occasions and I'm sure your repertoire hasn't changed."

"It has, but pain isn't one of them. So what do you think?" Oh, he did say that it was important to his wife and that could be one of the reasons why she left him, that, and a boyfriend."

"What do I think? I think that you have to be careful, Gerry. I think that as a good friend it's the only advice I could give. If he was just checking to see if you were like the others and he didn't want you to be, then that's all right. But, if he was checking to see if you liked doing that and he wanted you to join him in whatever, then you have a big problem. Which ever it may be, please be very careful, I love you; you're the closest friend I have."

The double order of fried calamari arrived and was unceremoniously placed on their table. Unlike "D'Arco's" or Ken's "Vincent's," the ambiance at *The 546* was created by its clientele.

"I could have gone with a single order; they must have killed one of those giant squids," said Gerry.

"It won't go to waste, what you don't eat I'll eat."

"How do you stay so skinny? I go to the gym three times a week and do my pilates at home and I'm always watching what I eat. If I didn't do all of that, they would be hanging a bell around my neck and sending me out to graze."

"You're in good shape, Gerry, don't sell yourself short. *She wanted to say, don't make it so easy for the wrong people.* By the way, I do walk though it's not a planned exercise. Oh, and I have a treadmill."

"It's not set up, Roni."

"Yeah, but I have it."

They had ordered a bottle of cabernet because they didn't intend to join the crowd at the bar. The calamari was gone and the bottle was a little more than half done as the back tables began to fill up with overflow from the front. The loud talking of someone emphasizing his importance near their table caused Veronica and Gerry to look in that direction. He was sitting at the next table with two other men and two women. The three men knew each other and were trying to impress the two women who they did not know. He was talking loudly about this deal and that deal while all of the time looking at Veronica and Gerry.

"Do you see what I mean about Bill? He's self assured, like you, and has savoir-faire. And then there are jerks like that…oh my god he's motioning to us!"

"You girls want to join our party?"

"No thank you, we're just finishing up here and then we're going to meet our husbands," said Gerry.

"Very well put," said Veronica in a whisper.

"Aw, come on over anyway and finish your wine here."

"I SAID…" Veronica put her hand on Gerry's arm. Gerry changed her tone, "No thanks again, we're having a private conversation before we go home."

The loudmouth turned away from them and directed his obnoxiousness to the two women at his table.

"Where is Ken when I need him," said Gerry.

What? To tie them up and stick needles into them? Veronica thought.

When they went to leave, Gerry looked back and noticed the "the mouth" as they named him, giving Veronica an x-ray.

∾

On Saturday, Veronica sent Gerry off with a litany of "being careful" and a promise to call her at the office on Monday. She then set up her treadmill.

❧ CHAPTER NINE ❧

On Monday morning, Bill was her first call. He could feel her hastiness, which he believed to be work related and, therefore, squeezed the entire itinerary of the trip into three minutes. She accepted a lunch date with him, which made her feel better for being so abrupt. Gerry's call quickly followed Bill's and she told of her weekend. Veronica surprised herself by having the patience to hear Gerry out. The auditors were due in after lunch and this would be the first time she would be facing her old team or, in this, case firm.

Bill was waiting for her at the front of the building.

"You look swell but, then again, you always look good."

Veronica was wearing an above the knee grey skirt and dark stockings. The stockings she would normally have worn with this skirt were ruined putting them on this morning and she hoped that she could get away with the dark ones on this unusually brisk day in May. It looked like another year where winter would go right into summer without a spring.

The tables in the restaurant were close by but somehow the conversations were kept private. Each table seemed self absorbed or at least felt that way.

"I called Ken and he said he would call Gerry about this Saturday night. You still do want to make this trip to the Cape don't you?" Bill asked.

"I'm sorry, I have these auditors coming in this afternoon and this is the first time since I left that firm that I'll be dealing with them. I've surprised myself by being so uptight about it. I'll be fine; it's just that I want to make a good showing."

"You don't have to apologize to me, Veronica, I fully understand. Accounting does this to people. It's constantly changing and laws and rules from just five years ago are obsolete. So don't apologize, I've been there. We can get through this audit, I know you can."

He was so sweet to say we. I want to care the same way and be able to express those feelings back to him.

"Thanks for being so understanding. You know, I've never been to Cape Cod. I don't know the first thing about it."

"Has Gerry been there?"

"No, she's never been there either. We're a couple of rookies as far as Cape Cod goes."

"Ken and I spent every summer there as kids with my aunt and uncle. When my aunt and uncle moved to Florida, we used the cabin with our wives. We used it together and apart knowing the key was hidden in the post. I didn't have any kids, but Ken's nephews and nieces enjoyed the river a lot with their kayaks and radio controlled boats. They were planning on having their own family; it's too bad they broke up. Ken's a good guy so maybe it'll be Gerry's gain."

Your wife disappeared and his wife divorced him. Is this the reason I feel the way I do? He explained it, there wasn't any intrigue. I have to stop this way of thinking.

"Is the cabin really a cabin," asked Veronica.

"No, we call it a cabin but actually it's a small house. It has two bedrooms, one bath, a living room and a kitchen. It's very well taken care of so let it be known I'm not bringing you to a log cabin."

"I'm going to be nicer, Bill. I've been too impatient lately and I'm going to change and not let my business interfere with my social life." *She lied about her business being the reason.*

"I didn't notice, Veronica, but if you want to be nicer than you are, if that's possible, then I won't stand in your way."

Gerry's right, he's so nice and I have to stop reading anything else into it.

He walked her back to her office and kissed her lightly at the front entrance.

"I'll call you before Saturday to make sure everything is a go with Gerry and Ken," said Bill, while still holding onto her shoulders.

"Thanks for taking me to lunch; I'm looking forward to hearing more about the Cape."

She tried to mean it and hoped he would take it that way.

∞

The auditors were prompt and Veronica was ready for them. Sal, the lead auditor, kissed her as she came out of her office. This was not the usual greeting from independent auditors but Sal had known her since she was first hired at Herzog & Herzog.

"So, how is Carney & Company treating you?"

"Just fine, Sal." Under her breath she said, "You shouldn't have kissed me. It's not very independent of you."

"And just how many opportunities does an old geezer like me get to kiss a dish like you? I'll tell you, nil to none."

Salvatore Pastore was still dashing at 62 years old and appeared fit in body and mind.

"You look great, Veronica. How's the world treating you?"

"Thanks for the compliment, Sal, I can't answer for the world, but I can say that I'm being treated very nicely. Today has been a very complimentary day for me." *For luck, I should tear my stockings more often.*

"Good to hear that," said Sal.

"I'll take you to the accounting department and reacquaint you with the manager and you can get started. You know the routine, same stuff different numbers."

As was their routine, they would be at Carney & Company all week.

On Friday, they wrapped up and Sal was the last to leave. He came into Veronica's private office to say goodbye.

"I'll say goodbye in here so we don't upset your office and I don't lose my independence." Sal winked as he said it.

He must have been quite a guy when he was younger because he's still good now. Gerry would have said this differently.

"Another thing, Veronica, besides how is the world treating you, is there anyone in particular that's treating you in a special way?"

"Yes, actually there is at the moment."

"Good!" Sal responded. "I hope he knows how lucky he is." At that, he kissed her and turned and waved goodbye again at her office entrance.

I don't want to give someone luck, I want to get luck. Maybe I have and I just don't know it.

∾

Gerry didn't stay over the next Friday night. She drove into Manhattan with Ken. Veronica assumed she would be seeing Ken on Friday night and maybe the rest of the weekend. She worried as to what Gerry had told her and was hopeful that it was the way Gerry thought. Gerry said it never came up again and that he didn't force her or suggest anything else that she would find uncomfortable. Gerry, not being able to hold anything back, certainly would have let her know. Veronica smiled at that thought and at the same time was worried.

Bill was the first to arrive and quickly remembered that he had left his overnight bag in his car at the parking garage. They would have to retrieve it after dinner.

Ken and Gerry arrived before Veronica had time to give Bill a glass of water. And not wasting any time, the four of them left to go to their favorite restaurant and meeting spot, D'Arco's.

Dominic brought them their menus and immediately was engaged in speaking Italian with both Bill and Ken. Veronica noticed that Gerry wasn't her bubbly self.

"Are you feeling okay, Gerry? You seem quiet, which is not like you at all."

"I'm all right, but are you saying that I'm a loud mouth? Gerry was smiling.

"Now I know you're all right. But, to tell you the truth, I'm not too sure as to how *I'm* feeling. I think it's this see saw weather that we're having. Everyone's coming down with something and there is all sorts of coughing and hacking going on in my office."

Dominic took their order to the kitchen, returning only to serve their wine.

"Now for Cape Cod," Bill announced.

"Since it's the Memorial Day weekend, everything will be available to us. All the restaurants will be opened and there'll be a full boat schedule to either Nantucket Island or Martha's Vineyard. We could go whale watching or there's a small island where we could watch the seals. And then there are the lighthouses. We could go to the Chatham Light at night. It's a great spectacle." He looked at Ken who shook his head in agreement.

"What about scuba? You had mentioned it." Gerry asked.

"Sure," Bill responded. "Bring your suits."

The entrée arrived and the conversation dwindled to a halt. As they were finishing it up, their conversation resumed.

"Always good here!" Ken exclaimed.

"Is there something wrong?" Bill directed his question toward Veronica who had just picked at her food.

"It's certainly not the food. I was telling Gerry that there are a lot of colds or flu going around in my office and in my building. You ride the elevator with people who sound as if they should be in bed. If I am getting something, I should be over it by next weekend. Right now I'm not all that bad; I just don't have my normal appetite." Veronica looked over at Bill who, thinking ahead to the evening, looked deflated. It didn't make her feel any better.

Dominic arrived at their table along with the bus boy who was cleaning up the empty plates. "Any one having dessert?" Dominic said in English. He took three orders for tiramisu while Veronica opted for cappuccino.

"So, any questions about next weekend?" Bill and Ken almost said in unison.

"You guys have known each other too long. Do you both think alike?" Gerry asked.

"No we can't," said Ken. "He's the thinker, I'm the stinker." He laughed as his own self-deprecating humor.

"Are you okay, Roni?" Gerry interrupted.

Veronica had only sipped at her cappuccino and had turned ashen in color.

"I'm not feeling good at all. You're going have to excuse me, I'll be right back." She stood up, almost knocking over her chair, on her way to the restroom.

"I'll go with you," said Gerry.

"I hope there aren't any attendants," said Veronica.

It was open and Gerry locked the door behind them.

"I'm sorry, Gerry." She knelt before the open toilet and vomited. Gerry held her hair back and placed her hand on Veronica's forehead.

"Don't be sorry, you've done this for me more than a couple of times during our history together."

Gerry helped her up to her feet and over to the sink. Veronica proceeded to wash her face while, again, Gerry held her hair back.

"I don't look so good," said Veronica looking at her reflection in the mirror. Just as she spoke she felt the tide coming back in and she was back at the open toilet.

When they got back to the table, Gerry announced that they were going back to Veronica's apartment. She looked at Ken and told him that she would be staying with Veronica and asked if he could bring her bag out of his car. Bill knew that his bag was not coming out of his car.

"I'm sorry," Veronica said to Bill.

"Don't be sorry, just get yourself better for next weekend so that I can show you a good time."

Ken had gone for his car and now handed Gerry's bag out of his driver side window.

❧

In the morning, Veronica was feeling better and talking about breakfast.

"Are you sure? After last night, you cannot possibly have any insides left."

"I can't thank you enough. And thanks for staying with me. Did you put my clothes in the laundry bag?"

"Yes, I did and I see that you're shopping right out of Vogue these days. What happened to Victoria?"

"When I have someone to dress for, I'll be back to Victoria."

"You do have Bill! You do remember those guys from last night, the ones who didn't get laid." Gerry laughed.

They went out for breakfast, but not before Gerry called Ken to tell him that she would see him tonight. Gerry ordered a large breakfast which included both eggs and pancakes while Veronica ordered a meal that she could finish, eggs over light and toast.

When they returned to the apartment, the light on the answering machine was flashing. It was Bill asking how Veronica was feeling. She hadn't called him.

"I know, Gerry, I'm working on it. I'm going to treat him better. Speaking of the boys, you seemed kind of quiet earlier, is there anything wrong?"

"I wasn't going to say anything but since you asked, he did bring up that S&M stuff again. He said it in the context of talking about his wife and girlfriend. I said it didn't have any interest for me and he said he was glad. Is he hung up on this because he was burned, or does he want me to do it? I don't know. Everything else is great. He doesn't force me to do anything." Gerry shrugged her shoulders.

"In my case, maybe I just don't know how to accept relationships. Bill's wife disappeared, as I had told you, and beyond that, he seems much more normal than me. Maybe this coming holiday weekend will answer all of my questions. As far as you and Ken go, I'm surprised you haven't flat out told him *no way*."

"You're right, it's easy for me to act that way when I don't care. But the real me isn't that tough when I like someone."

Veronica nodded her head and they said their goodbyes with a hug before Gerry entered the subway entrance.

❧ CHAPTER TEN ❧

Their trip to Cape Cod began at 6AM. It was already close to 70 degrees with solid blue skies. Bill drove his SUV into Manhattan and picked up Veronica and Gerry; then drove to The Bronx to bring Ken on board. Gerry had taken the Long Island Railroad into Manhattan Friday night, keeping her car safe at home. Ken had doughnuts ready and four cups of freshly brewed coffee which he brought with him in the SUV. Four hours later they crossed the Bourne Bridge. Bill did all of the driving.

As they came off the bridge, Bill and Ken explained to Veronica and Gerry what a rotary is and how germane it is to Cape Cod. They also noted the American Indian names that were also associated with the Cape and how this compared to Long Island. Gerry had already noted the comparison to the Hamptons at the east end of Long Island.

"Except that the look of the Hamptons goes for just about the entire Cape," said Bill. He explained that their destination was Mashpee, again, of Indian origin.

The houses on the road were in contrast to each other. Some were in the million dollar category while some looked like shacks in comparison.

"Don't let the looks of those *shacks* fool you; depending on their location, they will probably sell for a million. The owners, like my uncle, have different reasons for not selling but, when they do, they'll be demanding big bucks. My uncle's not for wanting money is our gain." Bill drove the big SUV into a short driveway between a large contemporary house and next to a small weather beaten cottage.

"That's the Cape Cod look, those shingles. The residents here want their homes to look that way. You won't find many aluminum sided houses as you do on Long Island. Another thing the year round residents don't like, are those big contemporary homes. They want every house to look like a cape style home."

Veronica and Gerry were the first out of the SUV.

"This brings back a lot of great memories," Bill said while looking at Ken.

"What's that nice smell?" Gerry asked.

"It's the mulch, that red stuff you see around the plants and bushes."

"It looks pretty and smells good," added Veronica.

Bill lifted the post and removed the key. He opened the door, and with a sweep of his arm, motioned them to enter the house.

"This is nice, musty but nice," Gerry said.

"There's no AC here so help me open all of the windows and we'll send that musty smell away," Bill said. He pointed out the bathroom for Veronica and Gerry, who during the last half hour of the trip, were asking for a pit stop.

Veronica chose the front bedroom leaving Gerry the rear one. Bill and Ken brought in their luggage, including the scuba gear.

After using the bathroom and settling in, Veronica and Gerry strolled outside and were awestruck by the setting of what they were now calling the cottage as apposed to the cabin.

"Look, the water's right here!" Gerry exclaimed. "I mean, it's right here!" She pointed to the end of the back yard and a dock leading right into the river. "Do you grow those big rocks here?" She added.

"No," Bill answered Gerry. "They were left here by the glacier, like the one that went through The Bronx and left all of those huge boulders. And boulders are what they're called."

"You seem quiet, Veronica," said Bill.

"It's the trip, and I'm probably still not a hundred per cent from that bout with that stomach virus. But I'm all right, don't worry, I'm here for a good time."

Ken suggested that they "cool it" for awhile; he'll make coffee and have the sandwiches he packed and discuss what to do first.

"Good idea," Bill said.

It was unanimous that it would be seafood for dinner. Their plan was to go to Hyannis and see the Kennedy Compound and the JFK Museum. After dinner in Hyannis, they would go to Chatham walk around the town and into its shops. By then it would be dark and time to see the Chatham Lighthouse.

"I think this is more than enough things to do consider-ing this was a traveling day." They all agreed and couldn't wait to have lobster for dinner.

∾

Bill drove by the Compound and asked if they wanted to get out and walk, since they couldn't get too close with a car. They said yes and Veronica and Gerry spent the next twenty minutes peeking over fences and through bushes. After walking the main street of Hyannis and going through the JFK Museum, they decided on a restaurant by looking at the menus posted outside.

They had four orders of clam chowder, which was pro-claimed as award winning, and four orders of lobster. Ve-ronica saw karaoke being set up in the bar area.

"I love listening to people sing and no, I don't sing."

"Maybe we could stop here on the way back from Cha-tham?" Gerry asked for Veronica.

"Sure we can," said Bill.

It was dusk and would be dark by the time they reached Chatham.

Bill drove through Chatham on the way to the lighthouse, leaving the walk around the town of Chatham for the way back. The road became a hill on the way up to the lighthouse. Near the top of the climb they could see the sweeping of the light across the sky. And as they reached the top, the sight of the glancing light across the water lived up to its description and cause Veronica and Gerry to say that the trip was worth it. Bill stopped the SUV in the parking area and explained that down below in the darkness was a beach. They stepped out to get a better view.

"This is really spooky," said Veronica. "And the night here seems a lot darker than on Long Island."

"It's because you don't have the amount of lights; not street lights and not city lights," said Bill.

"I knew you were going to say it was *spooky*," said Gerry.

"Can't help it, it's my word," said Veronica, grinning.

Because of the hour and because they were all tired from the drive to the Cape and at the Cape, they voted to go back Mashpee and their cottage. At the cottage, Ken produced two bottles of wine, which they took outside to the back patio. The bottles emptied, Bill said he was tired and went into the cottage.

"Look at those stars, I've never seen them so beautiful," said Veronica.

"Am I a fatalist or why do I feel that these good times won't last?" Gerry said.

"I'm not going anywhere," Ken answered by holding Gerry around the waist.

The wine was finished and the three of them found Bill sound asleep on top of the bed. Veronica took a sheet from the linen closet and placed it over him, while Gerry and Ken went to their room. She freshened up in the bathroom and then, after strategically placing a pillow between them, laid down on the bed. She had put on light pajama pants with a matching top. Veronica slipped under the sheet and listened to Gerry and Ken in the next room. They weren't muffling their actions, which caused Veronica's mind to switch from sleep to desire. She was as oblivious to Bill as he was to her and was not part of her fantasy. Her hand found the waistband of her pajama bottoms. She moved to the edge of the bed and dropped one leg over the side of the mattress. It wasn't long before the waves of pleasure came over her. The sounds from the next room subsided and she hoped that she had not contributed to their silence.

∾

Veronica was up first and made coffee from the special pot which Ken bought. She put in the gourmet coffee beans and enough water for eight cups, pushed the button and it ground the beans and produced the coffee in five minutes, complete with aroma.

"This is great, I have to get one when we get back," she said to Ken as he emerged from his bedroom. She looked across the river from the back yard and smiled, "And Great River looks *great*." She motioned with her head to the coffee maker and he nodded yes. She poured him a cup.

"When we were kids, Billy and me came up here from New York and had the best of times. Looking at the turns my life took, maybe there were none better. Billy's aunt and uncle were tops and made me feel like I was their nephew, too."

Veronica looked back at the river, "I hope we didn't bring all our gear for nothing. I really don't mind if we can't fit it in, but look at that! How often in your life are you going to get an opportunity to experience this and if we could get out there, it would be a topper."

"I'd like to go with you and I've gone in there many times, but I just don't feel right this morning and I don't want to risk the rest of our time here by getting sick," Ken replied.

"Tell me about it," said Veronica. She finished her coffee and went to go back to the bedroom as Bill appeared. "Hey, how are you feeling? I thought you died last night," she said.

"I'm sorry; I used to do this trip and still had plenty of gas left in me *and* the car to return in the same day. I was younger then; I'm sorry about last night."

"You don't have to be sorry for being tired, but if you think you owe me something, how about going for a dive?"

They had coffee together, Bill his first and Veronica her second. Bill ate a left- over doughnut while Veronica went to put on her suit. Standing on the dock, Bill explained that it's pretty deep right from the "get go" which was good for his uncle's sail boat.

"There are boulders lining the river by the cottage. This is not consistent with the rest of the river because my uncle had his part dredged when he put in the dock. This was done over fifty years ago. Individual dredging couldn't be done today because of shellfish laws, among others. He rolled down the boulders for support. Ken and I had names for them. "Devil's rock," "flat rock," "duck rock," you know, kid names."

Veronica could see she had better skills than Bill. The water was clear and free of sediment; a safe dive, not more than ten feet. He pointed out all of the childhood rocks and drifted back in time with each one. When they got back both Ken and Gerry were having coffee out on the patio. After taking turns in the bathroom to remove their suits, they joined them.

"Last doughnut," Ken exclaimed.

Veronica shook her head no, so Bill took it.

"So where are we off to today?" Gerry asked.

"How about we go over to Nantucket Island," Bill replied.

"I've never been there, and Roni?" Roni shook her head. "Then I guess it's virgin territory for us. A new frontier!"

Veronica looked at Gerry over her sunglasses. Bill and Ken showed no reaction. *Gerry's being good.*

"I'll go and get the ferry schedules from the car," Bill said. Ken went with him.

"Sooo, were you doing your pilates last night?" Gerry grinned..

Veronica blushed, "What about Ken?"

"He was too preoccupied."

"I know that I keep harping on the same thing, but I didn't miss him last night."

"I guess not," Gerry replied.

"I'm serious, Gerry, try to be serious too."

"I am serious."

"All right, you want to play that game. What about your Mr. Sam, "Mr. Sam the Vibrator Man," did he make the trip?"

"Okay, truce," smiled Gerry.

"He's an awfully nice guy, Roni. He went in the water with you when he really didn't want to, and… he'll do anything for you. But, it's your call and I'm not exactly the right person to be giving advice."

"But you are. He's nice and I'm giving this long weekend a chance at seeing things right."

Gerry nodded her head toward Bill and Ken returning with the ferry schedule.

They arrived in Hyannis with plenty of time to park the car and not have to run to the ferry. Bill and Ken paid for their respective tickets declining Veronica and Gerry's offer to buy.

"We're going over on the fast ferry. It takes only an hour to get there," said Bill.

"It's a catamaran," noted Gerry.

Bill seemed impressed and Ken shook his head with approval.

"You know," said Veronica, "We're not without skills."

Veronica and Gerry remarked that the ride over was very smooth and if they weren't looking out a window they wouldn't know if they were on the water. Inside, there were cushioned seats set around tables. The pilot's area looked like something out of Star Trek.

"We could just as well be sitting in a lounge," said Gerry.

They glided past the Brant Point Light and were soon walking up the cobble stones of Main Street.

"These stones remind me of Boston Post Road in The Bronx, said Ken.

"Do you know how they got here?" Gerry asked.

Before any one could answer she said, "The cobblestones were brought here as part of a ship's ballast."

Veronica's face showed amazement and disbelief of this first-timers knowledge. Bill and Ken, however, were impressed.

Gerry continued, "And did you know that at one time Nantucket and Martha's Vineyard were part of the New York colonies?"

"Let me see your hand, the one behind your back," asked Veronica.

Gerry showed her an empty hand.

"It's my other hand, which has the little booklet with my windbreaker draped over it, that you're interested in."

Veronica laughed and said, "It's not that I don't think you're capable of learning that stuff, it's just seemed funny that you *knew it*"

Ken took hold of Gerry's hand and she moved closer to him as they continued their walk up Main Street.

Bill put his arm around Veronica and she felt as if it were the arm of a stranger. She came close to having sex with him, maybe he thought they had, and yet his arm seemed like a foreign object. *There is definitely something wrong with me, she thought.* They had lunch at The Captain's Restaurant and, after spending over three hours on the island, turned back down Main Street to take the ferry home. Veronica and Gerry each had made purchases and their arms were full. At 4PM the temperature had dropped and their new Nantucket windbreakers were put on. Bill, on the way back, had taken Veronica's hand. *Again she didn't feel a connection.*

The ride back was as smooth and a little quicker than the trip over.

"We're going with the water," Bill explained.

∾

Back on Cape Cod, they chose to have dinner in Falmouth before returning to the cottage. Ken drove back to give Bill a break and Veronica snuggled next to Bill in the back seat. She was trying, and believing, that she could like Bill a lot better. By the time they reached Mashpee and the cottage, she was trying to convince herself that she was heading in the right direction. It was 8PM; Veronica and Gerry took the first showers followed by Ken and Bill.

Gerry and Ken went off to the back room. Veronica turned off the ceiling light in her room while she waited for Bill to come out of the shower. She slipped into bed wearing a tank top and pajama shorts, nothing special. Emotions began to wash over her; feelings of discomfort, mingled with no feelings toward Bill. She could feel the sweat on her brow.

Bill came out of the bathroom wearing nothing but boxer shorts.

"I've waited for this all day," whispered Bill.

"Me too," she tried.

As he moved closer he propped himself up on his left elbow.

"Could you please turn off the table lamp?"

"Sure." *That's an odd request.*

Veronica reached behind her to the night stand and turned off the lamp. As she was bringing her hand back, it swiped the top of the stand knocking one of her earrings off. It slid under the bed on the dusty hardwood floor. The interruption caused her to stop the process.

"Nuts! I'm sorry, Bill." *I'm going to be sick, I can't do this.*

"That's all right; I'm not going anywhere."

Veronica got out of bed and, kneeling down, reached under. Her hand closed around a small dust covered ring. It was happening again, just as it had over twenty years ago. She *saw* the imagery coming in short bursts one frame at a time. *There was a girl on this bed choking and then something about a river, then it became dark.* Veronica was frightened.

The ring was thrown hard against the floor under the bed. She rolled over onto her back saying, "No...No...No..." The overhead light was switched on by Gerry after she and Ken had heard Veronica call out. Bill was kneeling on the bed looking down at Veronica, who was lying on her back. Gerry went to Veronica, grabbed her robe from the foot of the bed and wrapped it around her.

"What happened, Roni?" Gerry begged.

"I don't know, I was reaching down to get my earring and all of a sudden the room started turning," she lied. "Right now, I'm very dizzy. I guess I really haven't shaken that flu bug yet," she lied again.

Gerry helped her to sit up on the bed and then she laid her back, keeping her robe on. She got a cold wash cloth from the bathroom and placed it on her forehead. Veronica allowed all of this to be done for her.

Something went terribly wrong in this house, maybe even in this bed, she thought. *I DON'T KNOW THESE PEOPLE! And maybe my sixth sense has been right all along.*

The morning could not have come too quickly for Veronica, who spent the rest of the night lying on the sofa with Gerry sitting right next to her. She apologized to Bill for ruining his evening; he had retrieved her earring. *She wondered if he had found the ring. I must keep up appearances,* she thought. The ride back to New York was like the ferry from Nantucket, faster on the way back.

Bill waited for Gerry to get her things from Veronica's apartment and then drove Ken to The Bronx and Gerry back to Long Island.

Veronica said goodbye to Bill who escorted her to the doorway and gave Gerry her clothes and a hug.

"Are you going to be okay, Roni? Do you want me to stay?"

"No, you just be careful, I'll call you right after I find out what went wrong with me."

Veronica closed the door, sat down in her favorite chair and was still there when she awoke in the morning.

❧ CHAPTER ELEVEN ❧

"This is the operator, how may I direct your call?"

"Have I reached the New York Police Department?" Veronica asked.

"Yes, how may I direct your call?"

Why can't they just say who they are, what's the secret?

"Could I speak to a... Detective Nick...Nicholas Vito, please."

"Let me look that up for you."

There was a pause.

Maybe I'm foolish to do this. I should just hang up.

"That would be Manhattan North, I'll connect you," said the operator.

There was another wait and Veronica pondered again. *I'm going to hang up the phone, no one will ever know.*

A harsh and grating sound jolted Veronica.

"Manhattan North, Schwartz!"

"Detective Nicholas Vito, please?"

Maybe I should think of some one else, she thought, and then was interrupted again.

"This is Detective Vito," the voice said. A voice that was as familiar as yesterday.

"Nick? This is Ron….Veronica Labrador."

It was Nick Vito's turn to be shaken by a voice. A voice that he thought he would never hear again.

"Wow! I'm not usually at a loss for words, but this is definitely one of those times. How are you? Where are you? Is everything all right, Roni?" *I don't even know what I'm saying or how to talk for that matter. Calm down, Nick!*

The way he spoke her name, so easily, she thought.

"I'm good, thanks, but I think that I have a problem and I didn't know who else to turn to. I've seen your name in the paper several times and, well, I just didn't know who else to ask. Maybe I shouldn't have bothered you"

"No, no you did the right thing. I'm glad you called, Roni, and I hope I can help. I'm working out of mid-town. Are you close by?"

"I'm working and living in the city now. Maybe we could meet, say outside of Rockefeller Center and do something low keyed like coffee? It's difficult for me to explain it over the phone and, actually, I wouldn't want to."

Why was she avoiding saying his name? She wondered.

"If three o'clock is good for you, I'll meet you outside of the main doors," said Nick.

"That's good for me," Veronica replied.

"Good then, I'll see you there, Roni." *I can't stop saying her name.*

ॐ

Veronica delegated her work to her staff to free up her afternoon. She also visited the executive rest room three times before leaving at 2:50 PM to meet Nicholas Vito. Her nerves were getting the better of her and the weather didn't help. It was an unusually hot day for June and winter had gone right into the summer, skipping spring.

Nick was staring down the sidewalk in the direction from which Veronica would be coming. The walkways were busy as usual, groups of unrelated people melding with each other through the common activity of walking. Some moved quickly and others were strollers, being passed by the more determined pedestrians.

Nick stood gazing at her for an instant until he realized who she was. Veronica was cutting her way through a bunch of tourists and Nick's heart reacted with his recognition. She was taking long strides on moderate heels and was wearing an above the knee dark blue straight skirt with a white silk blouse. Her straight hair bounced slightly in the light breeze. Everyone else on the crowded sidewalk had disappeared except for Veronica Labrador.

"Roni! You look as good as if you were still walking the hallways of Armstrong High."

"As good?" *I think Gerry's rubbing off on me.*

"Better," he added, grinning.

She gave him a quick hug and a slight peck on the cheek. Nick feigned not wanting much more.

They walked side by side to a nearby coffee shop. Once inside, Nick pulled back a small wooden chair for Veronica to sit on. She smiled her acceptance as Nick took a seat opposite her, at an equally small table. The waitress displayed her disappointment at their "coffee only" order. Nick couldn't keep from looking at Veronica and hoped he wasn't caught staring. And that his eyes weren't giving away what was in his heart.

"So you're a detective, that's great."

"And you're a CPA, that's not too shabby either."

"Whick school did you go to?" Nick asked. *As if he didn't know.*

"I went to C.W. Post," she answered.

"So you stayed on the Island?" *He knew that.* "I went upstate New York to SUNY Binghamton and after that I got into this cop thing. I like it, I really do."

The coffee was served and this relieved them from making further conversation. They looked at each other and smiled, as he brought the plunger down on their coffee brewer.

"You can do it next time," Nick said. *I shouldn't have said "next time."*

Veronica smiled and took a sip out of the cup that Nick had poured.

"Tastes good," she said.

Nick waited to see if Veronica had more to say and, as the awkward period continued; he dropped both hands palms down on the table.

"Do you feel as strained at this as I do, Roni? I'm glad you are who you are, but I probably would be doing a lot better if you were a stranger. You know what I'm saying?"

"I know," Veronica replied. "It's like we were divorced or something."

"We were in a way," Nick said nodding his head. "Look Roni, let's treat this like a business; I'm a detective with the NYPD and I'm here to listen. Begin your story at whatever point you want to. I don't have to know every personal detail, I only have to hear what your problem is. In other words if you have any little secrets, you can keep them to yourself."

"Thank you, I really mean it. Do you remember Gerry McCabe?"

"How can I ever forget Gerry," Nick responded. "She was more than the life of the party, she WAS the party!"

They both laughed.

Veronica explained how they met Bill and Ken and how they decided to spend the weekend on Cape Cod at Bill's uncle's place. She purposely skipped the prior intimacy with Bill. Almost as an afterthought, she told him of Bill's wife's disappearance, that there was an investigation and that they had been going through a divorce. Nick's eyebrows rose on this disclosure. Veronica just shook her head at realizing her own stupidity.

"Now I have to tell you about a very spooky thing." *He remembered so well her attachment to the word, "spooky."* She folded her hands, but did not divert her attention from Nick. "Back in Armstrong High, when I found out about you and Andrea, did you ever wonder how I came upon this?" *I'm still not saying his name, why?*

"I did, Roni, but it was not the most important thing. What I *did* was." He thought he saw her swallow nervously.

"Well, and this might be tough to believe, I got that bit of information from her ring."

"Huh? From her ring?"

"Yes. She showed me her ring and handed it to me. When I took it from her, well I *saw* you and her together."

"I…I don't understand?"

"The only way I can explain it is that it was like a slide show. I saw what happened to the wearer of this ring or what they had done. I've never told anyone this before. Not Gerry, not my parents, no one until now. Other than my own, I haven't touched another person's ring until last weekend. I'm not an expert in this but maybe a traumatic event or what some one is thinking about is transferred to their ring. I don't know."

Nick *was* staring and, at the same time, listening intently to Veronica. He didn't know what to ask and could only continue to listen, in order to learn, so that he could ask questions. He leaned on both arms which were on the table wrapped into each other.

She told of their arrival on Cape Cod, the drinking of the first night and an abbreviated version of sightseeing the following day, leading to Sunday night. Veronica explained that she had just gotten into bed when she reached over to the nightstand for the light. *She did emphasize that she had just gotten into bed so that he knew they had not had sex.* She knocked her earring onto the floor and, when she went to retrieve it, she brought up a ring. She then had the same reaction as she did that morning at Armstrong High.

"I *saw* a woman being choked and then there was something about water and then it became dark. There is a river in the back of the house." She told him of Gerry and Ken in the next bedroom and that Gerry had come to her aid. It was Veronica's turn to stare at Nick, to see what reaction he had to both her weekend romp and to her ring disclosure.

He didn't show any emotion at either. Inside, Nick was more relieved that her weekend was cut short without sex and less amazed at her ring abilities.

Nick took out a small pad and wrote the names of Bill Vito and Ken Small. He chuckled at having the same name as Bill. Veronica had their telephone numbers which he also recorded.

"I'm not too sure about the addresses."

"It's all right, the telephone numbers will do. And now that I'm thinking about it, because of the guy's same last name, I was told about this missing person case from Long Island. I didn't follow it, though; he's no relative of mine."

She didn't tell him that Bill had also disavowed any relationship. *That conversation seemed so long ago.*

"I want you to be careful with this group, Roni."

"Do you believe me?" She interrupted.

"Yes I do, I have personal proof."

They stood up from their tiny table.

"I'll be careful. I'm finished with them and I told Gerry to be careful too. Thanks for believing me and, oh, thank you for the coffee."

"No problem, Roni. I'll call you."

Outside of the coffee house, there wasn't any physical contact between them; they waved goodbye and left as they had arrived, without attachment.

❧ Chapter Twelve ❧

Nick called his counterpart in Nassau County, Long Island.

"Marvin Grossman here!"

"Marv? This is Nick Vito."

"Hey Nick! Been a while now. How're they hanging?"

"I've been good, thanks, hope the same by you. Look, Marv, I have a situation where I need some information for a friend."

Marvin Grossman knew that *friend* meant this was not an official request.

"See what you can get me on a Bill or William Vito, no relation, and a Ken or Kenneth Small. Supposedly, the Vito wife disappeared two years ago. At the time they all lived on Long Island.

"I remember that case well. Especially since you shared the last name of her husband, who I recall, came up clean. Do you have something on that?"

"Like I said, it's for a friend. If it leads to more than that, you'll be the first person I'll call."

"Thanks, Nick, I'll get back to you."

"I thank you, Marv. You don't owe me any thanks."

"Yes I do. You gave me my only touchdown, just as you had said you would."

"You don't have to keep thanking me for that. You were the only one open."

"No I wasn't. I was so slow that you scrambled around until I got into the end zone and then threw me a perfect pass. What was it, fifty yards in the air?"

"I heard it was one hundred yards," Nick answered back.

"Well whatever, it was a great moment for me."

"Thanks for the memories; I'll talk to you soon, Marv."

Nick hung up the phone and thought back to that day when, after the game, he still had the love of Veronica Labrador.

❧ CHAPTER THIRTEEN ❧

Bill left messages on Veronica's answering machine at the apartment and with her secretary at the office where fortunately for her, she was at a late lunch. She didn't want to speak to him and yet she knew that she would have to.

"Veronica! I have Mr. Vito on the phone." Her secretary called over.

Which Vito?

"Hello?" She answered without emotion.

"Veronica! I've been trying to reach you all week. Are you okay?"

"I'm sorry, Bill, we've been real busy here with the fiscal year ending June 30th. We're making sure all the numbers are properly reflected. You know how that goes."

"You're speaking to me as if I were in your classroom. You don't sound as if everything's all right?"

"No, no. It's the job and I'm still not over that flu bug that did me under."

"Then I guess this weekend is out."

"I'm afraid so. I'll be going out to Long Island to visit my parents and staying over."

"Then I'll call you next week?"

"Please do, thank you."

"I'll talk to you then, hope you're feeling better."

"Thanks, I'll speak to you then."

This phone call wore me out, I can't do this again, Veronica thought.

∾

"Veronica! I have Mr. Vito back on the line again."

This time she thought quickly. "How did he ask for me?"

"He asked to speak to Roni."

"Thanks, I'll pick up."

"Hello, how are you?"

"I'm okay, Roni, how are you today?" *Did she seem happy to hear from me?*

"I just heard from the other Vito and it wore me out."

The good news is that she's tired of him and the not so good news is that she may not be happy to hear from me either.

"You do whatever you like, Roni. You don't have to string him along for anything legal or otherwise. I think there's something fishy here, but that's me. I'll have some more information for you in a little bit. While we're on the subject of going out, is there any way you might want to have dinner with me this Saturday?"

"I don't think I'd be good company right now, so I don't think it's a good idea."

"Is it less not being good company or more not a good idea?"

This caused Veronica to laugh. "That's the first laugh I've had since this all started. I'm not sure what you just asked me, or what answer to give you, but I'm going to be honest with you; my emotions are all jumbled up. I lied to Bill Vito and said that I was visiting my parents this weekend, but now I think I will."

"How are they?" Nick asked.

"They're both doing great, still active. You know, I never told them."

"No I didn't know that."

"I didn't tell them the reason, the how or the whys. You were the son my father never had. He thought he'd be rooting for you in the NFL."

"I thought of him in the same way; he was at all of my games and my own father wasn't. Maybe if I had spent more time paying attention to the game instead of watching you cheer, I'd have made the pros."

"You broke all of the school records, what more did you want?"

You, but he didn't say it.

"I'm doing what I really like, Roni. And I can't ask for more than that out of life. When I get something back from Nassau County, I'll give you a call. This way we can make it a business dinner. Say hello to your parents for me."

"Thanks, I will."

∾

On Friday night, while Veronica was packing her clothes for her weekend on Long Island, Gerry called.

"Hi Roni, I'm returning all of your calls. Are we still friends?"

"I called you about five times this week and you never called me back. Does this mean we're breaking up?" Veronica said, answering Gerry's question.

"No, it may mean that I'm getting laid," said Gerry giggling.

"Why do I even try to have a normal conversation with you?"

"Because you love me, that's why."

"And you take advantage of that. Let me know when the normal conversation flag is up."

"Whose flag is up?"

"See, that's what I mean. I called to tell you that I spoke to Nick Vito."

This news stopped Gerry cold.

"Okay, I'll be serious now. How did this happen? Did he call you?"

"No I called him. It's about a matter concerning the guys we're seeing. I can't explain it over the phone but I want you to be very careful."

"Is there a problem with Ken?"

"I don't know."

"Roni! You don't know, but you called in the cops?"

"I didn't call in the cops, I called Nick."

"That's the same thing, he's a cop."

"Gerry please, I can't explain it over the phone, it's too complicated. Are you going to be on the Island over the weekend?"

"I'm spending the weekend with Ken." Gerry answered tersely.

"You can reach me at my parent's home until 5:30 PM. I'm taking the 6PM train back to New York. I can explain everything." Veronica pleaded.

Gerry ended with, "If I'm back on the Island before that, I'll call."

Veronica knew she would not be hearing from Gerry.

❧ CHAPTER FOURTEEN ❧

Marvin Grossman left a message for Nick that he wanted to see him and Nick left a message at his Mineola office that he would be on Long Island on Tuesday. The meeting was set for 10AM by their intermediaries.

"Hey Nicky!" Grossman held his hand out, "How long has it been?"

"Four years maybe," Nick responded. "At the funeral?"

"Yeah that was it." *He knew it was at the funeral, he just didn't want to say it.* Grossman's eye's lowered and then rose. "How's little Nicky?"

"He's great, Marv, thanks. He makes it all worth while. I've been doing it with nannies and unbelievable neighbors, but what he really needs is a mother. You know what I'm saying?"

"He's almost four then?"

"Yeah, he was just four, July 25th."

"Time passes unannounced, doesn't it?" Grossman said.

"That's very poetic. Is this the new Marv?"

"No, I'm not a new Marv, but I do have some new news for you. Take a seat while I provide you with some eye opening details."

Grossman opened a manila folder on his desk.

"Back in 1973, there was a scandal with the New York Yankees. It seems that two of their pitchers swapped wives and lives. It naturally, caused a huge uproar."

"I don't remember, Marv, and neither do you. We were both around nine years old. What are you building up to?"

"Hey, this is my show and, besides that, you know how much I like theatrics."

Nick nodded his head and said, "On with the show."

"Well, it seems that Billy here and Kenny took a page from the Yankees play book. They swapped wives. This all came out when Clarice, who was Bill's wife, I hastened not to use his last name, disappeared."

"Thanks," said Nick.

Grossman went on, "It seems that after two months, Kenny's wife tired of the arrangement with Bill, you know who."

"You're enjoying this, aren't you?"

"Yes I am, shall I go on?"

"Please."

"Now, Ken's wife applies for a divorce. For the record her name is Justine and is currently teaching school on the Island. Clarice and Justine–great names, okay I'll continue. Clarice likes it with Ken because they're both into sex with pain. They're both happy with the musical chair partnership until Clarice ups and vanishes. We check Billy and Kenny out. No money to gain, no insurance policies, nada. They're both clean, except, we got a missing person. And that's where it sits two years later. Can you add anything to this torrid tale?"

"Being in this business, I don't know why I wouldn't have expected something like this, but your file opened my eyes. I would say something about your presentation but I won't because I want us to remain friends."

They both laughed.

Nick continued, "If I have something to add to this case, like I said, you'll get it right away. How about getting some lunch, my treat?"

"Sounds good to me," said Grossman.

✖ CHAPTER FIFTEEN ✖

Nick was sure the information he received would be upsetting to Veronica and asked if could meet her at her apartment Wednesday night. Afterward, they could go out for their "business" dinner. When she answered the door, her appearance caused a feeling of lightness in Nick's heart. She had on red silk slacks with a matching short jacket. Nick was also dapper, in a black sport jacket and tan slacks.

"You look fabulous!"

"You look good, too. Would you like something to drink?"

"Ice water will do. Thanks."

They sat on soft chairs opposite each other with a coffee table between them. Veronica brought his water.

"I went to Long Island yesterday and I have some information you might find both interesting and upsetting." Nick went quickly. "It seems that Bill and Ken were involved in wife swapping and some kinky sex."

Veronica's hands went immediately to her face, covering her eyes. Nick was glued to his chair physically but mentally he had his arms around her. She held her hand up as Nick started to rise from his chair.

"I'll be okay, really, I'll be fine. I feel so embarrassed and stupid." *She wanted to say, especially around you.*

"You think you're the first person that was ever placed in this situation, Roni? Not so, I see it every day. Good honest people caught up in things that no one could ever believe would be true."

"Thanks, and thanks for being so diplomatic. If you wouldn't mind, could I get a rain check on our dinner for tonight? I have a lot to sort out and I feel as if I lost my appetite. Could you call me this week?"

"Sure, I understand. I'll call to see how you are."

She went with him to the door and they lightly hugged.

After Veronica closed the door, she could no longer control her emotions. She walked away from the entrance and wept loudly. Nick, who had not moved away from the closed door, heard her anguish. He went slowly down the stairs, fighting to control his own emotions.

❧ Chapter Sixteen ❧

Veronica had another busy week in the office and away from her desk. And, again, was not there when Bill's calls came in. She knew that sooner or later she would have to face Bill and that was exactly what Veronica wanted to do. She didn't want a night date, where she would feel vulnerable. She wanted to set the time and place, which she did. Gerry had not called.

"Hi Bill. It's Veronica."

"How are you stranger? Are you trying to avoid me?" Bill quipped.

"How about having lunch today down at the coffee shop?" She didn't answer his question, which was not lost on him.

She sounded very formal. "Okay, down at the coffee shop it is." *He couldn't keep from answering her in the same stilted way.*

Bill was standing inside the entrance of the shop when Veronica arrived. She greeted him as she had done with Nick. A short exchange of physical contact; a hug, peck on the cheek and now they were both seated at a table by a window. Veronica relied on *ad lib* rather then saying something that sounded like a script. She at least owed him that. As she was staring out at the noontime strollers trying to put her thoughts into words, he spoke, startling her with the first volley.

"So, I guess that's it for us? I can see what's happening here, I'm not stupid."

"I …I think so, Bill, I don't want to string you along with you thinking we're going forward and me feeling we're at a standstill. For me, it's all chemistry and emotions and I don't feel they're right with us. I'm sorry. I could tell you all of the nice things about you, but I don't want to patronize you. You'd be great for anybody but me. It's me, what can I say." She stopped talking, purposefully wanting him to put in the final nail. He looked hurt.

"In other words, this is it? No other times together? Just like that, end of story?"

"Please, Bill, it has nothing to do with you. I've felt this way for a while and it has me emotionally drained, which has now made me physically sick. That's what happened to me on Cape Cod. My emotions boiled over to a point where I can't go on."

He took all of this in while looking into Veronica's eyes. She hadn't noticed in all of this time, how piercing *his* were. It was fifteen seconds before he spoke again; it seemed to Veronica much longer than that.

"I'm going to give you a break from me and than I'll call ….."

Veronica interrupted, "I don't think that is a good idea, Bill. You said it; it's the end of the story, our story. I tried, and you were always more positive but, in the end, this is the only way it can be."

"Your way!" said Bill.

"Yes, if that's how you want to look at it, then yes, my way and only my way." Veronica was up for the task and getting better.

Bill stood up from the table and placed a ten dollar bill on it. "Let this be my final investment in this relationship." He looked at Veronica with those newly discovered piercing eyes, nodded his head and left.

Veronica was both exhausted and relieved. She was so at ease that she was able to finish her Reuben sandwich and then relax with a second cup of coffee. Her stomach, which had been giving her so much trouble, was knot free.

After lunch, the office routine went smoothly and she didn't flinch whenever the phone rang. *Time to hit the single bar scene, she thought. She then thought of Gerry.*

∽

Back in her apartment, Veronica made supper for one and decided she had nothing to lose by calling Gerry.

"Gerry?"

"Roni?" answered Gerry. "Thank you for calling. I was going to call you, but you've always been the better person. I'm sorry, Roni. And don't you say you're sorry too because you've got nothing to say you're sorry for. I do. I'm going to The Bronx tonight; maybe tomorrow we could get together?"

"That would be nice, Gerry." *She wanted to say, please be careful.*

"I'll have my car, so I'll be driving in from The Bronx," Gerry added.

"That's great; I'm looking forward to it."

"See you in the morning, Roni, have breakfast ready."

"I will," said Veronica. *She didn't mention her meeting with Bill.*

Veronica went to bed after watching late night television. She slept soundly for the first time in a long time.

∿

The telephone's ringing was blended into her nonsense dream until it had rung enough times to demand attention on its own. Still trying to separate the dream from the ringing phone, Veronica answered groggily.

"Hello?"

"Roni …"

Veronica knew what her name sounded like and knew it was Gerry trying to make the sounds. Other words followed, but they were garbled.

"Gerry is that you?" She glanced at her digital alarm clock, it read 2:15 AM. "What's wrong?"

"Roni!" She was crying. "Roni, he beat me. He tried to tie me up. He raped me Roni, he raped me." Gerry was crying uncontrollably.

"Where are you? Where are you, please tell me."

"I'm at Our Lady of Mercy Hospital in The Bronx. I…I drove myself here."

"Did you tell them what happened?"

"I did and I think they've called the police."

"Good. I'm getting dressed; I'll be there as soon as I can."

"Th…thanks, Roni."

∞

"This is Detective Vito!" Veronica had used Nick's direct line.

"Nick, I just got a call from Gerry, she was …raped by Ken Small." Veronica was choking back tears as she spoke. She told him where Gerry was and that the police had been alerted.

"I'm on my way there now, don't you worry, Nick comforted. *That was the first time she's used my name.*

❧ CHAPTER SEVENTEEN ❧

Nick went past the usual array of nurses, orderlies and technicians, but this time there was also police activity in the hospital. And there was always that antiseptic odor. Both of his parents had died in hospitals and he knew that smell all to well.

"Hey Vito, you got some senator's kid in here?", some one called over, kidding Nick about his high profile cases.

He went over to him and in a low voice told him that he was here for the same reasons as his team was. That Gerry McCabe in that room over there was a personal friend. They shook hands and Nick went into the room.

She was lying in a fetal position facing away from the door.

"Gerry," he said softly.

She heard a familiar voice call her name and turned very slowly in its direction.

"Nicky, Nicky," she called out. She tried to cover her face with her right hand, which wasn't attached to the intravenous. He took her hand in his and kissed it. Her lips were swollen, she had a welt under her right eye and her nose was probably broken. Nick patted down her matted hair, knelt down beside her bed and kissed her forehead. "Please don't cry."

"What about you?" she asked.

"Me? This is normal, I cry over commercials," Nick answered. "You don't worry; everything will be fine. You came to a good hospital. Please just hang in there."

"Nicky?"

"What?"

"She never stopped loving you. She just doesn't know it."

"Me neither, except I *do* know it."

Gerry tried to smile.

"Thank you for that," he said as he kissed her forehead again, and left.

Nick came out of the room and spoke to the officers milling around. He was assured that the suspect was Kenneth Small.

"Give me fifteen minutes before you go pick him up." They knew what he meant.

"Okay Nick, you got it."

∾

Nick drove through the deserted Bronx streets with vengeance in mind and arrived at Ken Small's apartment in less than ten minutes. *I hope that bastard's still there, he thought.* He parked his car across from the apartment and crossed the street. A figure in dark clothing came out of the building and went toward a parked car.

"Kenneth Small?" Nick called out. The person stopped. Nick did not and kept moving ahead. By his silence, Ken had identified himself.

"I'm detective Nick Vito NYPD. We have a woman in a hospital that I believe you know. She says that you beat her up and worse. We're, at this moment, verifying her information." Nick kept talking and closing the distance.

"Oh, so you're that *guinea* cop friend of ..." Nick had closed in too fast and Ken saw what was about to happen. He swung his right fist at Nick's head. Nick moved back, kicking the side of Ken's knee and at the same time grabbing his right arm as it missed him, swinging by. Ken dropped to the ground with his right arm pulled behind his left shoulder and Nick's knee on the side of his face. He was lying on his own left arm.

"If you don't give me your left hand, I'll pull this arm the rest of the way out of its socket." His left arm came around and Nick cuffed Ken from behind. Still forcing his knee into Ken's face, he said, "I just came back from the hospital, you piece of shit, you're a real big tough guy with girls and wimps. You beat her up, a ...a beautiful girl like that." Ken started to talk. "Don't you fucking say anything," Nick leaned harder with his knee. The uniformed police had started to arrive. Nick stood up, pulled Ken to his feet and turned him over to them.

❧ CHAPTER EIGHTEEN ❧

The following week, on Thursday night, Veronica and Nick had their first date since Armstrong High; even though they both were calling it a business dinner. This time, Nick had a chance to look around Veronica's apartment.

"It's definitely Roni! Every thing's so neat and all in its proper place. It does look good and so do you." *He wanted to say that she was stunning, the prettiest girl in New York and on and on, but felt he did not have the* right *because of what happened over twenty years ago.*

"You look good, too, Nick," she said, and was surprised at how good it felt saying it.

She was wearing what Gerry said was becoming her uniform, a skort and blouse combination. Yesterday, Veronica took a vacation day to be with Gerry on her first day home. She was surprised to find out that Bill had visited Gerry while she was in the hospital.

They sat next to each other in a steakhouse that Nick had chosen. It was across town and Nick had used his own car, finding a space nearby.

"Parking spaces in the city are part of the benefits of being a cop." Nick volunteered as he opened the door for her. He was going to say, *nice legs*, except he didn't have the right.

After they both ordered wine, Veronica was the first to speak.

"Due to circumstances beyond my control, you've got to know a lot of stuff about me and I wonder if you would like me to catch up with your life?"

"Sure, but let me start you off with the most important post-Veronica event. I have a little boy."

Veronica was startled and surprised to have had this news strike at her emotions.

"How ...how old is he?"

"He's four."

"What's his name?"

"It's Nicky, what else?"

"Were ... were you ..."

"No, his mother and I were not married. She was a cop like me and, right after Nicky was born, she was killed on the job in an auto accident. The only good part is that little Nicky was too young to understand."

Veronica looked into Nick's soft brown eyes, unlike the piercing ones of Bill Vito. "You just gave me question block if there is such a thing."

"Well then I'll just have to answer questions you might have asked. Let me see ...I live in Queens in a row house, I bought it new. I have great neighbors, who help me with little Nicky, and that's about all there is in my life away from the job. On the job is another story and the more that I've been thinking about it, the more I want to ask for your help."

Veronica was puzzled. "In what way could I help?"

"If you've been reading the paper, there's a missing little girl from a well-to-do family. I'm afraid that the ending to this story is not going to be good; however, the family does want and need closure. This is where you come in. The girl's tiny gold ring was found outside her bedroom window. I know this is a lot to ask, Roni, but I'm asking."

"If you think that I can help, I'll try, even though I've never done this on demand, it's been accidental."

After dinner they skipped dessert and went back to Nick's car. "You're going to see a little of the backdrop of a police department. I'm taking you to the evidence room."

∾

Nick worked his way through the building, with Veronica at his side. They went past the Desk Sergeant and down a hallway. At the Evidence Room counter, he asked for the Ellis case. A small box was handed over and Nick signed for it. He motioned for Veronica to follow him and together they went down a small hallway with doors on both sides. Nick opened one of the doors and guided Veronica inside. It was small, a little larger then a walk in closet. Nick set the box down on a waist high shelf that went around the room. He lifted out a very tiny gold ring in a plastic sleeve.

"I'm afraid, Nick….I don't want to touch it."

"Roni, it's okay, you don't have to." He put the ring back in its protective pouch and back into the box. "It was wrong of me to involve you in this, I'm sorry. We can go …"

Veronica had taken the plastic sleeve from the box and spilled the ring into her hand. She immediately dropped to her knees. Nick stood back watching, not wanting to break her concentration.

When she stood up, Nick again, waited for her response.

"I can describe the person who took her, Nick."

Nick didn't waste any time in calling for an artist to sketch Veronica's description.

"There's something else, I think she's alive. I can't explain it, I just do. I can't *see* her alive, I just don't *feel* that she's dead."

"I hope you're right. It certainly isn't the ending I thought this case would have. Those poor parents, they're already prepared for the worst. It will be a miracle."

As they waited for the artist to arrive, Nick's optimism for this case was dampened by the thought of what Veronica must have seen that day in Armstrong High.

∾

The police artist was there in less than thirty minutes. As he sketched and the rendering became a face, Nick's focus increased. "That's Ellis' brother-in-law. I questioned him. He lives in Brooklyn."

Nick asked Veronica if she wanted to wait for him here or he could arrange for someone to take her back home. "I could call you if it looks like an all-nighter."

"If no one minds, I'd just as soon wait for you here."

"I don't think anybody is going to mind, Roni."

∾

It was all over by eleven o'clock. The brother-in-law was booked. Little Stacey had been reunited with her parents, with Nick bringing her to them. It took all of three hours, guaranteeing that Nick Vito would be back in the morning papers. When the brother-in-law was brought in, the sight of him jolted Veronica. She had never laid eyes on him and yet she had.

She asked, "Why did he do it?"

"He says that the child is his and that's all he'll say until he speaks to his lawyer. Nothing surprises me anymore."

Nick looked at her, not wanting the evening to end.

"How about getting a night cap? I don't want our business dinner to end with my business. The place is right around the corner from here."

"I know about around the corners in this city. Okay, one drink and you can take me home." *Why did I say that, I really do want to go.*

❧ CHAPTER NINETEEN ❧

They left Nick's car at the station house and walked fifteen minutes around a few corners. Jimmy's Pub served food at the bar and was well known for its brisket of beef. But, foremost, it was a cop bar; a place to wind down from seeing the worst that society had to offer. It was a place to enjoy the company of those who understood why it was their job to be in the wrong place and at the wrong time, again and again.

As Veronica and Nick came through the entrance, calls for Nick came from all sides. She could tell that he was well liked.

"Hey Nick! It's karaoke night! How about it!"

"How about what?" Veronica asked.

"I'm a big star here," kidded Nick. Don't you remember besides football I sang in the choir and I had that little band?"

"Yes, yes, you did sing in the choir. And the band that never made it out of your basement. I remember that too."

"Well, all that hidden "talent" came together in this place."

They were seated at a small table near a small stage where there was a sign "Karaoke by Lynn." Lynn waved to Nick and he brought Veronica up to the stage to meet her. Veronica could feel the warmth and admiration toward Nick and knew it wasn't from any performance here.

Nick ordered Veronica her favorite, a strawberry daiquiri, maybe a first for Jimmy's Pub, he told her. Again there were calls for Nick to sing.

"How did you know I love to listen to people sing with karaoke?"

"I didn't."

There were more calls for Nick.

"Okay, okay, I'll do one tune. Then I'm going to sit down and enjoy my girl and my drink." He went to the stage to a round of applause. Veronica joined in with their chant of Nick! Nick! Nick!

He began, *"This heart of mine, been broken..."*

It was up-beat and, along with Veronica, the crowd clapped in rhythm.

"I love you, yes I do," he sang looking out at the crowd and *her. Enjoy my girl,* she repeated to herself. She stopped clapping and took hold of her drink. Veronica's lips were quivering and her eyes were welling up. *What is wrong with me? I've just been through too much lately.* She bit down on her glass letting the ice cubes touch her lips. Her emotional wave had passed. Nick was just finishing up and came back to their table, and to a smiling and applauding Veronica.

"You were great, Nick, you really were." Instinctively he grabbed both of her hands for his thank you. At the same time, the crowd was calling for *his* song.

"You have a song? You wrote a song?"

"Yes, it's not much."

"Well, they seem to think so. Could you do it, Nick? Please?

"Okay, but this is the last one."

Again there was applause as he went back up to the make-shift stage.

"All right guys and girl, this is the last one."

He began,

> *"When I see your name I can see your face,*
> *And I feel my heart aching inside.*
> *As the years go by I can't stop that feeling,*
> *of wanting you by my side.*
>
> *Life for me is not complete and though I pray,*
> *I can't erase the reason that pushed you away.*
>
> *I'm sorry for the pain that I caused you*
> *And I wish I could tell you that I still care.*
> *You will always be in my heart*
> *and this is my hurt to bear."*

Nick's voice took on a raspy quality giving the lyrics an emotional turn. This feeling spewed out to his audience and that's when Veronica heard from the bar in back of her and then around the room. "It's her!" This time Nick was looking *only* at her. *Nicky, Nicky,* Veronica grabbed at her glass, again, as he sang the refrain. *The ice cubes couldn't stop the flood.*

"It should have been our time to be happy
It should have been our time forever
It was our time of love."

Veronica was no longer in control. She was crying openly as Nick, the music still playing, left the stage and lifted her to her feet. "I've never loved anyone else," he said. "I'm so sorry that…" Veronica put her fingers to his lips. "Stop!" Between sobs, and trembling lips she found a will to say, "my love for you has stayed buried in my heart. It was the only love I've ever had. I love you, Nicky."

"I love you, Roni, I always have."

With their arms entwined around each other, they stood together as one.

When they regained their composure, one by one, almost like a wedding reception, Veronica was introduced to New York's finest. Veronica's right hand left Nick's only when it was needed to greet someone.

"This is Mike McLaughlin, we call him *super cop.*"

Veronica could see why. She judged him to be around 6'5" and had the weight to go along with it.

"Nice to meet you, Roni. We always knew that his song was for someone special. Now we know for sure. And don't believe that super cop stuff. After Nick here tackles them, I just sit on them."

"I don't buy that Mikey'" Veronica said uninhibitedly. "Something tells me you did a little more than that to earn that title."

Mike turned to Nick. "I like her!"

He proceeded to put a bear hug on the both of them. "All the best, I really mean it."

Veronica looked into Mike's glistening eyes and saw his heart, and why a place like this was necessary for them to have.

One more drink later, they said their goodbyes and left Jimmy's holding hands.

❧ Chapter Twenty ❧

"My neighbor is keeping little Nicky overnight." Nick volunteered.

Veronica coyly answered, "Now it's my turn to say, do you want to come up for some coffee?"

"Yes," Nick nodded. The drive without traffic was short; the traffic lights behaved and Nick found a space close by Veronica's condo, using his "right to park" ID.

Veronica unlocked her door and stepped in first. She swung the bolt and turned facing Nick. Their arms circled and drew them close, Nick's right hand behind her neck, Veronica's hand on the side of his face. Their lips were parted as their tongues within their kiss were actively bringing their bodies to another level. Their eyes met and answered any questions as to the path they were on.

Nick undid the zipper of her skirt, letting it drop to the floor. With Veronica's help, they twisted loose the buttons on her blouse, pulling it behind her and down off her arms. Her body was silhouetted against the dimly lit apartment as she led Nick to the bedroom. He removed his clothes as Veronica pulled back the bed's coverlet. She had purposely left on her bra and panties. While lying side by side, he lay back, moved Veronica on top, and unfastened her bra.

Nick reached down his left side and held her panties out as she brought her knee through, leaving them on her left leg.

"I love you, I love you," Nick whispered.

"I love you," Veronica repeated.

Her breasts felt good against his chest and her hard nipples added to his own excitement.

Nick gently lifted her up then down. There wasn't any resistance as he entered her and she began to thrust forward and back for both their pleasures. His moan signaled his ultimate satisfaction and he stayed within as she used him for hers.

The sandman was put on hold as they returned to their desires another time before falling to sleep in each other's arms.

In the morning, Veronica called her office and told them she wouldn't be coming in. Friday was Nick's day off, anyway. Veronica made coffee, but not before they were once again back on her bed. Later, they decided to go out for breakfast. She slipped on her sweats; Nick was limited to his same clothes.

The place was small and only opened for breakfast and lunch. They sat at a counter and placed a duplicate order for two fried eggs and bacon on a roll.

"I need a shave, or I'm going to give you more than a *glow*."

"Can I go with you? I want to meet Nicky."

"That would be so good, Roni. He is really a great little boy."

"I'm sure of that, and there are some other people that I'm sure would like to meet him and you too, my mother and father."

"Your parents, I'd like to see them too. As I said, after you, your father was my biggest fan. We have the whole day, Roni."

"And night," Veronica winked.

❦ Chapter Twenty-One ❦

After breakfast, Nick drove them to Queens, New York, by way of the mid-town tunnel. The attached houses were nice and neat and all in a row, as if made by a cookie cutter; all with five steps leading to the front door. He pointed out his house before going over to his neighbor's home and little Nicky.

A woman answered the door holding a young child.

"Hey Nick! Tough night?" Dotty looked at Veronica, who was standing next to him. *Dotty ignored her temptation to say guess not.*

"Not really. Dotty, I want you to meet Veronica; I've known her all my life. We lived in the same neighborhood and went to high school together. And we now kind of found each other again."

Dotty placed the child into a baby seat as Veronica extended her hand. Dotty took it and covered it with her other hand. "I sense a certain chemistry between the two of you. My husband says I'm psychic."

"Maybe because we were in the same chemistry class at Armstrong High," Nick quipped.

Dotty gave Nick a *look* over her eyeglasses and motioned them inside. She looked at Veronica and said, "He IS funny."

"I know. It's all part of that innocent makeup that I love." Veronica replied.

Dotty moved them through the house, "Nicky's in the den watching television."

The love remark was not lost on Dotty.

"Daddy!" Nicky went from the TV into Nick's arms.

He was dressed in blue shorts, white two button shirt, white crew socks and white sneakers.

"I want you to meet a good friend of mine."

Adorable, Veronica thought.

Veronica knelt down, "Hi Nicky, my name in Veronica."

"You're pretty!"

Veronica smiled, "Thank you, Nicky." And then chuckled, "Boy are you your father's son or what?"

She put her hands on Nicky's shoulders; it brought him forward and he put his arms around her neck. She held him close and looked up at Nick, whose eyes betrayed his emotions.

Nick took Dotty over to the side and paid her for her time. In the beginning she had to be forced to take any money, but since her husband had been injured *on the job,* the wives of his fellow officers had been bringing meals by each night. And *this,* Nick told her, was his way of doing his share. He overpaid her.

෴

Nick showed her around his house, with Nicky running from room to room.

"It's as neat as I would have expected it to be, Nicky."

"MY name is Nicky!" Little Nicky exclaimed.

Veronica laughed. "You're both Nicky, see, you're just like your daddy."

Little Nicky was pleased.

"You just scored double points." Nick said.

CHAPTER TWENTY-TWO

Nicholas Vito hadn't been back to the old neighborhood on Long Island since his parents had died and certainly not to Veronica Labrador's house since high school. They went past the little league baseball field and its tree covered parking lot. It was one block from her house.

"Remember that lot?" asked Veronica.

"Absolutely! It's where we did our imitation of a pretzel."

"I don't know what you're talking about," pouted Veronica.

He stopped in front of her house. It was de-ja vu for him as he took in the familiar and, at the same time, the changes. Veronica took Nicky out of his car seat.

They had called ahead and Charles and Diane Labrador were waiting at their open screen door. Later today the forecast was for over 90 degrees and this door would be shut and the air conditioning would be on. Again, Nick saw the familiar and the changes. They were both seventy years old.

"We missed you son," said Charles as he went past Nick's hand and gave him a quick hug and a pat on the back. Nick kissed and hugged Diane who willingly returned his affection.

"It's been a long time. All the bushes and trees – all that I remembered have matured and gotten old." Nick remarked. "Me too," he added. "You both look great."

"And who do we have here?" Diane brought herself down to Nicky's size.

"I'm Nicky".

"And we are Diane and Charles, Veronica's mommy and daddy."

"My mommy died."

Diane, although having been given Nicky's history, was still not prepared for his response. She swallowed hard and held him close.

"Your mommy will always be watching over you from heaven and keeping you safe."

"Do you think I could visit her?"

"Right now she wants you and your daddy to be happy."

"I could be happy if I could see her."

"Oh, you will someday."

Diane kissed him on the top of his head and stood up as Charles lowered himself to take her place. He asked him about sports while Diane could be heard in the kitchen blowing her nose.

Veronica turned to Nick. "Nicky has so much love in him and it just reflects the kind of love you have shown him. You've done a great job, Nick. I'm so proud of you."

❧ CHAPTER TWENTY-THREE ❧

On their first day back to work, Nick met Veronica for lunch.

After they ordered sandwiches, he noted her troubled look and asked, "What's up, Roni? Is there something wrong?"

"I spoke to Gerry this morning; she says she's a lot better and thinking of going back to work. She's taking the train into the city tonight and is staying over, so I'll see for myself. Gerry did say that she's seeing Bill. I didn't say anything back, should I have?"

"You did the right thing. I'm sure you didn't want to push her away again. You made me a believer, so I'm already convinced that something happened in that cabin and that the river may hold some answers. If you want, In about two weeks, I can get three or four days off and we can take a mini vacation. Can you do it?"

"I think so." Veronica nodded.

Nick took a sip of coffee and continued. "We won't have to be involved in the discovery, if there is a discovery. I'm working on that, so don't worry. Did I mention we're going to re-visit our scuba diving skills?"

"Scuba diving?" Veronica asked.

"Yeah, I'll rent a boat and we'll renew our teenage distractions."

"Distractions?" Veronica asked again.

"Yes, from ending up, parked under the trees, at the little league baseball field."

She playfully swatted Nick with her paper napkin.

They both took a chewing break with Nick finishing first.

"I think we both figure this victim to be Bill's wife, who was last sleeping with Ken."

Roni didn't speak, but shook her head in agreement.

"It could be one of them and it could be neither of them. When they were doing the missing persons investigation, the cabin wasn't listed on the check list because it belonged to Bill's uncle. No one knew of it. The cabin might not tell us too much now, but the body, if it was down far enough, might give up the murderer. Another piece of this puzzle that's in our favor, is that the last two summers since Bill's wife disappeared, have been unusually cool. By the way, Ken, who's living on Riker's Island, may be getting out on bail. His lawyer's working on it."

"Do you think he'll get out?" Roni asked concerned.

"Yeah, probably, that's the system, but don't worry, we can get orders of protection for Gerry and you, too."

Nick walked Veronica back to her office and they embraced at the front of the building.

He held her by her shoulders, "Thanks for letting me back in."

"Thanks for my song. The door was never closed."

∿

The train was on time and Gerry was let in by the doorman. She didn't make note of him.

Veronica was waiting at her opened door.

They hugged outside of her apartment and when they let go, Gerry volunteered.

"I'm okay. I'm good."

She was right about her face, it was fine. But, there was something else, Veronica thought.

"Do you want to …"Veronica didn't get to finish.

"No Roni, could we just have something here?"

Roni made a quick spaghetti dinner.

"It's good, Roni."

"Thanks." Veronica waited for more.

"I don't have happy moments like before. Where everything before was funny and a joke, nothing's funny now. Bill is trying to work me through it. He's good for me right now, and I might be good for him, too."

Veronica let her continue.

"He *does* have some of his own issues to work through. He really liked you, probably even loved you, though he wouldn't say that to me. Let's face it, you were like winning the lottery."

"Oh please, Gerry, it's not the cover, it's the story that counts. My book already had a leading man and I have never been this happy, EVER," Veronica emphasized.

Gerry continued, "I told him that you and Nicky were joined at the hip a long time ago, when you were both fifteen; that it had nothing to do with him. I know he's attracted to me, but I guess I'll just have to wait and see. I *am* a realist."

Veronica felt she was finished. "Look, how about we get out of this apartment and all of this heavy conversation and get a drink like the old days, or at least, the old days of a couple of months ago."

"Okay, all right, let's go," Gerry said.

Veronica noticed a brief spark in Gerry's eyes.

∾

"The 546 Restaurant wasn't crowded and they took two stools at the center of the bar.

"So what'll you have my pretties?" Johnny the bartender was always "on."

"Compliments will get you places." Gerry exclaimed.

"And what places are we talking about?"

"Not that place and if you keep looking at my legs, don't charge us for the drinks."

"You're funny and pretty. And, I happened to be looking at your skirt. It reminds me of a cheerleader; or maybe I want it to remind me of a cheerleader."

"It's just a pleated skirt, they're in this year. If I give you a cheer are the drinks free?"

"If it was up to me, yes, but it isn't, so it's no. Gerry and Veronica, right?"

"Good memory," said Gerry. I'll a have raspberry martini and she'll have strawberry daiquiri." Gerry turned toward Veronica.

Veronica nodded yes.

"A raspberry martini, that's new." Veronica gave Gerry a quizzical look.

"It's my new image – class. Bill has been taking me to places that I would like to get used to. I feel safe with him…

no, I feel comfortable with him. There was always an edge when I was with Ken. And you're not going to believe this one – we haven't had sex. When we kiss goodnight I can feel that he wants me. He says not to worry; when you're ready I'll be there. He's giving me time and, for the first time in my life, I need it more than sex. So what do you think of all this stuff? Notice I didn't say shit."

"It all sounds great. He treated me well when I was with him and was never out of line. We just weren't compatible. Does he ever mention his wife or Ken?" *There, I've said it now we'll see.*

"Funny you should ask that. Last night he mentioned both of them. He told me that they did a crazy thing and switched or swapped wives. Did you know that?"

"No I didn't." Veronica lied.

"He said there wasn't any chemistry between him and Ken's wife, but that his wife and Ken hit it off real good. He thinks Ken and his wife had something going before this stupid, his word, *idea* and that he and Ken's wife were duped. He said they were tricked into being stupid. Before she disappeared, he hadn't seen her in months. He's opening up to me and I want to believe him,"

"It sounds like he's trying hard to be honest with you." *I wonder why he's giving this up now. He never told me any of these things.* "If you're asking my opinion, he seems to understand that going slow with you is what you want. The last thing you need now is to have some inconsiderate jerk bring you to where you don't want to be. Go with it. You're happy, nothing wrong with that."

"Another thing he said was maybe he needed to know you in order to appreciate me. What do you think he meant by that? I didn't ask him."

Veronica watched Gerry's eyes glistening with tears. *My God she is really stretched out. That bastard Ken!*

"Maybe he meant that whatever physical attraction he had toward me, doesn't measure up to the emotional feeling he has as far as you're concerned. I know that's the way it has to be for me. Look, Bill has a great personality, is good looking, but he couldn't get into my heart. Nick was already there."

The mention of Nick's name caused Veronica to become emotional.

"I can't say his name without getting like this. Look at us, two hot chicks crying in our drinks like a couple of drunks."

They both laughed and wiped there eyes at the same time.

In the morning, Gerry left to go back home and Veronica left for work and, later, lunch with Nick.

❦ CHAPTER TWENTY-FOUR ❦

Two weeks later, Veronica and Nick worked out a four day vacation break. During these weeks, little Nicky had visited the Labradors three more times, and now would be staying with them, while Veronica and Nick were away. Charles and Diane were planning their days around him.

Little Nicky was taken to the Labrador's the night before they left. The next morning they packed Nick's car. It was late August and the sun was already putting on a strong appearance.

Nick heated the frozen bagels to have with their coffee. Because Nicky wasn't there, it was her first time in Nick's bed.

"You need a new bed or at least a mattress. It's too hard on my back."

"No problem, I'll lay on my back all of the time."

Veronica playfully slapped him.

"I'm not talking about that and you know it, I'm talking about sleeping. Is this going to be an official trip?" Veronica changed the subject.

"No, this is actually Marv Grossman's missing person's case. You remember him?"

"Yes, I do. He was *so* funny in school. He's a cop?"

"Yep, he's a detective and he's still funny and still sloppy. I don't know how he finds anything on his desk."

Nick paused.

"I don't know what I expect to find, if anything. And, if I do, and if this is more than a missing persons case, it would be out of mine and Marv's jurisdiction. It would become a Massachusetts problem. Got your scuba?"

"Yes, Nicholas, you've asked me this three times already. The next time I'm going to say no."

"Okay, you have your scuba gear – check."

"What about any hot outfits?"

"They're all hot after I put them on."

"Okay, hot body – check."

Nick locked the house and opened the car door for Roni, who was wearing a green tank top, tan shorts and white sneakers, no socks. Her hair was tied in a ponytail for the trip.

∾

The traffic going over the Throgs Neck Bridge was light and they were through New York and half way up the stretch of I-95 belonging to Connecticut in just under two hours. Veronica was thinking about her last ride up through here and how much, this time, it felt so right.

Cars were passing them as if they were standing still, but Nick kept the pace at a steady 65 to 70 miles per hour. Thinking back, Veronica smiled, as she drew a mental picture of him now, and then. He was wearing jeans and a white tee shirt and sneakers. His tan arms had filled out and his face and wavy black hair fit into his maturity.

"You have a joke that you want to share?"

"Yeah, I was just thinking back to how slow you used to drive when we were dating. I knew that you were trying to prolong our time, and I liked that."

"So you knew. And I thought that you thought I was just driving carefully."

"Well, there was a contrast on driving around and driving to the ball field. You did a little speeding then."

Veronica paused and looked out the window.

"Did we miss too much, Nicky?"

Nick looked at her and slowed the car. He stopped on the shoulder, in front of a sign declaring that the next exit was a detour for the following exit. There were cows in the nearby field. He put his emergency blinkers on.

"I…didn't plan…well I take that back, I did plan; just not here. That sign is appropriate, though. We took a detour…a detour in our lives. Detours avoid problems but they do bring you to where you want to be. And I don't want to be anywhere without you. Open the glove compartment, please."

Veronica opened the door and saw a small white box.

"Take it out, it's yours."

Veronica's fingers were trembling along with her lips as she removed the box cover and lifted out a black velvet box. She flipped it open to a small sparkling diamond set upon a gold band. She was crying.

"Will you marry me, Roni?" Nick was crying.

"Yes, yes, yes!"

They remained entwined until Veronica gasped that she needed air. When they stepped out of the car, the cow's odor hit them. They both laughed as they walked hand and hand around the car before getting back in.

"I wanted this to be romantic. I wanted it to be at dinner tonight. I…"

Veronica interrupted. "It was perfect Nicky."

∾

"How about a real breakfast," Nick asked.

"Sounds good, do you know a good place?"

"Follow me!"

Veronica giggled.

Nick turned off the highway at the next exit and made a couple of turns and went down a hill into a small town, still in Connecticut.

"I ate at this place a couple of times while I was taking a training course around here. The homemade pies are the best, but the French toast is unreal."

George's Diner was shaped more like a restaurant, except when you went inside; it then became a diner. The parking lot was crowded.

"We are getting a booth ready now or you can sit at the counter," said the hostess.

Nick looked to Veronica to make the decision. She chose the booth.

Five minutes later they were following the hostess to a booth at the corner of the diner. As if performing the *wave* at a sport stadium, the heads belonging to a construction crew sitting at the counter followed Veronica to their table.

She was oblivious to them while Nick, following behind, saw her in a different way.

They sat opposite each other at a freshly washed table and held hands. She was staring at her ring finger and its symbol of love.

"This is our first time out in public as an engaged couple. I…I just can't believe it. I…"

"Roni, please don't do this and get me started. They'll throw the both of us out of here." Nick kidded.

Veronica dabbed her eyes and let it pass.

"What can I say; you've given me the happiest tears of my life."

"Ahem." The waitress cleared her throat. "Can I take your order now?"

She looked at Veronica wiping her cheeks and Nick's watery eyes.

"Do you need a little more time?"

"No thanks, we're ready," said Veronica. "I'll have the French toast special and regular coffee."

"I'll have the same." Nick chimed in.

The hostess left and they had a good laugh at their own expense.

"You were right, Nick; the French toast was the best I've ever had." She looked down at her ring again. "I still can't believe it."

Nick placed the check on top of his money, and put a juice glass on top to hold it all in place. As they went out the door, the heads at the counter, again, followed her out.

"You stirred up the counter crowd in there."

"I can't help it, it's summer and it's hot and I left my *burkas* home; they weren't the right colors anyway. And besides that, biologically, for over half of them, I could be their mother."

"Would you want that?"

"To be their mother?"

"No," said Nick smiling, "to be *a* mother."

"I've always wanted to have a child. I just got to be a mother first. To have another child would make me very happy, but not any happier than being Nicky's mommy."

"Then I guess we'll have to start working on that." Nick said as he started the engine.

Veronica leaned over in her seat and put her arms around his neck.

"I love you so much."

❧ CHAPTER TWENTY-FIVE ❧

Three hours later, they arrived at their motel. After checking in, Nick helped Veronica up the stairs with her rolling luggage while hoisting his with his other hand.

"We're only staying three nights, what do you have in here?"

"You don't want me to wear the same clothes do you? And then I have to have some choices, so I have two of this and, maybe, this top doesn't go with this skirt, you know what I mean, don't you?" Veronica's eyes were smiling.

"Of course I do," said Nick. "I have the same problem with my tee shirts; some necks are rounder than others and…"

She pushed Nick onto the king sized bed and jumped on top of him.

"Now you were saying?"

"I was just saying that I hope you have enough clothes with you, or else I'll just have to buy you some so that your case is as heavy as mine. That's what I was saying."

"I thought so," she said in a pretend superiority tone.

He rolled her over and looked down into her eyes which drew him into her very soul. He lifted himself up. "We can continue this later."

Veronica reached up and pulled him back. "Why wait!"

∾

Veronica slid open the balcony door and stepped out into the breeze blowing up off the water. They had showered and dressed for dinner. Nick came up behind her and put his arms around her waist.

She looked over her shoulder. "You picked the perfect motel, Nicky."

Nick replied, "Except for maybe one thing, do you want to leave a suggestion that the shower be made larger?

Veronica laughed. "Well it WAS funny. No christening of the shower, but it will be something to howl about as we grow old together."

They drove to the Town of Falmouth and were lucky to find a parking spot on the main street. The town was crowded with out of state license plates. Veronica paused at each car to see where they were from.

"Look, Nicky! This one's from Alaska!"

Nick shook his head in appreciation of her enthusiasm. Men on the sidewalk were looking past their wives to get a look at her. And here she was oblivious of the commotion she was causing. No pretenses, no airs, she was her own person; not made up. *Nick thought, loving someone puts a fear in you of losing that person. I have to keep her safe so that my worst nightmare doesn't come true.* Nick shuddered at the thought.

After their lobster dinner at a small restaurant on Main Street, they walked the town before returning to their motel.

"It's a real nice town," Veronica noted.

They had gone out on the balcony again and were sitting with their feet on the railing.

"That's why I picked this motel; for the view of Vineyard Sound and Falmouth.

It's a real town, with year round stores. Not just tees and sweats for the tourists."

Veronica nodded in agreement.

"We better get to bed. Tomorrow we're going to rent a boat and try to find out what you saw that night. If the water doesn't give up anything, then I'll just let Marv Grossman know about the address, and leave it at that."

Nick went in first and Veronica followed him fifteen minutes later, but not before soaking up as much as she could of the lapping water; even though she could no longer see it.

She looked down on Nick, who seemed to be already sleeping. As she slipped into the large bed, Nick immediately awoke.

"Did the agency send you?" asked Nick.

"Yes, I picked the short straw for this gig."

This drew a laugh from Nick. "I guess you'll have to work on getting a longer straw."

"I'm not touching that one." Realizing what she had said, they both burst out laughing.

❧ CHAPTER TWENTY-SIX ❧

The boat yard didn't have many customers at 9AM. Veronica wore a sundress over her bikini, and Nick had on his long multi-colored swim trunks. They were both carrying black bags which held their scuba gear and wet suits.

Nick told the manager that he wanted to rent a Whaler for about three hours, who said that he'd be right back with the paperwork.

"Where did you ever get those swim trunks?"

"There is a story behind them. When I went shopping for new ones, I, of course, wanted maybe a solid blue; however, this pattern matched the one I could get for little Nicky. So now we match, even though he's not here and I look stupid."

"That's a nice story and I won't bring up those trunks again. Or, as Gerry might say, maybe down, but not up."

"What if I told you that the story is not true and I just brought these on a whim. Would it make any difference?"

"Please, let me believe the first story."

The manager returned with two teenage helpers who began ogling Veronica. Nick stepped in front of them, and they retreated back in the direction of the boat which they were supposed to be preparing. After receiving safety instructions from the manager and taking care of all fees, they were led to the boat.

"I'm impressed. When did you learn how to drive or steer or whatever you're doing with this boat."

"For a short period I thought that I might have liked to go with harbor patrol but it only lasted for an instant. I'm glad that I didn't choose it because I think I'd find it too restrictive. Oh, by the way, I would like to be addressed as Captain Nick."

"Ooh Captain Nick," Veronica said in a little girly voice, "what do you think of this?" In one motion she removed her sundress, revealing her tiny bikini.

"Now it's Captain Nick's turn to be impressed. Could you please bring me the ship's charts?"

"So now it's a ship?" Veronica stayed in character and sashayed over to Nick. "You mean these charts, Captain Nick, the street atlas of Cape Cod that you made me buy?"

"Yes, those are my charts. I estimate that it'll take about 45 minutes to get to where you say the cottage is."

"Well," said Veronica still using her little girly voice, "Captain, or is it now Commander, I'm just going to lie in the back here and soak up the sun, that is if that's all right by you."

"You're good to go and I'm going to keep my fat mouth shut."

"Roni, Roni! We're getting close to the mouth of the river."

"I…I must have fallen asleep. Where'd you say we were?" she asked.

"Do you see anything familiar?"

"No, no I don't, not yet."

"It's just ahead of us now. I'll be turning into it."

"Wait! That big tan colored house on the end; it's really close to the cottage."

Nick slowed the boat down and asked Veronica to get into her wet suit.

"While we're still in open water and not near any homes, this is a good time to do this."

She pulled it out of her bag and stepped out of her bikini.

"It's going to come off anyway when I take this suit off, so I might as well be comfortable."

"I didn't say anything. Can you come over here and take the wheel while I change?"

She took the wheel as Nick pulled off his large trunks. He looked over at Veronica.

"I'm not saying anything either, but I think you like me," she observed.

Nick turned out of the bay and into the mouth of the river.

"That's it, right there!

She was pointing to a small building sandwiched between two enormous houses.

"I recognize the back patio." She winced at her memory.

He stopped the boat in the middle of the river and set down its anchor.

"I don't see any activity from those adjacent houses. I'm not going to take any chances, so when we leave the boat, we're going to stay under until we get back. Maybe we won't be noticed."

They left the boat at the same time, without a ripple. Roni led the way to the edge of the river. She pointed to the boulders. Nick could see that they were in only one section. He motioned her to go no further, as he closed in on the boulders. When he reached the bank, he found Veronica at his side, pointing again, this time to a specific boulder. It looked to be flat, and seemed to be the bottom of some sort of crevice or cave. He went straight to it with his arms outstretched, and was able to get his body into it before coming up against a bag. It felt like a water bag in the water. He put his light right up against it and recoiled backwards. Even though they were here to find foul play, he didn't expect to find it inches from his face. He signaled Veronica to go back to the boat and he followed close behind.

He helped lift her into the boat and then hoisted himself up, falling sideways, over the railing and onto the deck against Veronica.

"I'm sorry, did I hurt you? My fins got caught on the side of the boat."

"No, I'm good. What did you see down there?"

"I saw through a translucent bag and at what I believe is human remains. I've seen a lot of stuff and, at the same time, I'm never fully prepared. I'm okay, and now we know for certain what you saw actually happened. When we get back, I'll call Marv Grossman with what I know; but not what we did to find it out. This will become a closed missing person's case for New York and a homicide case for Massachusetts."

They changed back into their original dry clothes and, as noon was approaching, returned to the boat rental pier.

&

"So what do you think?" Veronica asked.

They were dining in a small restaurant outside of Falmouth. The portions were exotic and small, which made Veronica happy. Nick needed more, so he finished all of the bread and the antipasto without any help from her.

"I'm thinking that there's no way that you and Gerry can stay out of this."

Veronica sighed.

"Besides the body, when the investigation team begins a sweep of the cottage; "reading" its contents and pulling together a picture of what might have taken place there, before two years ago and after, you and Gerry will be part of that *after*."

"So what should we do?"

"That's the part that I'm working on. Just how much can we give them without giving up the incident of the ring? I don't think that it's a good idea. Am I right?"

"Yes, I don't want to go there."

They both paused in agreement.

"Before we left for dinner, I called my parents to give them the good news."

"What'd they say?"

"I spoke to my mother. She cried. She said my father couldn't come to the phone right now."

"Great! Our kids have no chance. They'll be emotional wrecks in an instant."

"I wouldn't have it any other way; at least it shows they have heart." Veronica said.

"You're right again, what can I say? I'm no better."

CHAPTER TWENTY-SEVEN

After breakfast, while Veronica was freshening up in the bathroom, Nick made a call to Marv Grossman's private line.

"Marv, its Nick Vito."

"Hey Nick, how are ya doin?"

"Pretty good. Remember that Clarice Vito missing persons case? Well I got some update on it. I think that your missing persons case is closed and Massachusetts just got themselves a homicide case."

"How did you get that, Nicky?"

"I met someone who, with a friend, became "associated" with Bill Vito and Ken Small, and then became suspicious. Their names are Veronica Labrador and Gerry McCabe."

"What!"

"Yes, Marv, after all this time, I got a second chance. And to really bring you up to date, we're getting married."

"What! That's great, congratulations. Wow, I can't believe it. All the best!"

"There's more. Gerry was raped by Ken Small, who is now *away*."

"I didn't know. I don't read any New York City papers."
He looked at his desk, "I got enough papers of my own."

"I saw that, I can't believe you have a desk under all of
that."

"Okay, okay, haven't changed. What do you have for
me?"

"All right, here goes, there's a cottage on Cape Cod which
is in Bill's uncle's name. Veronica and Gerry were taken
there during their "association" with him and Veronica
"feels" that something isn't right. And another thing, along
with the cottage, check out the river. The cottage is right on
the water."

Nick gave him the location of the cottage.

There was silence on the phone.

"Something's not right here, Nicky. I know that I'm not
the sharpest tack in the box and I trust you more than anyone I know, but this is just too much information coming
from such a short "association." Don't you think? He didn't
confess to her did he?"

"No, no, no nothing like that. Look, Marv, you didn't
know about the cottage before so now you do. Go with
that."

"I'll call the State Police of Massachusetts. I got a buddy
there at the Yarmouth barracks. I won't ask you any more
questions. Let me see what I have here."

Nick listened to a rustling of papers and laughed to himself.

Grossman came back to the phone. "I got it here…Clarice
Vito, 5'9" and one hundred twenty five pounds. Tall girl! She
had long hair, a brunette…hmmm."

There was another pause.

"Don't worry; I won't give Veronica up too easily, Nick. She's too current, but if it happens, maybe they'll ask her a couple of questions and that'll be it. I can even run interference, and tell them that I covered any questions of him telling her something pertinent to the case. I did in a way by asking you. In any case, she and Gerry will have small roles."

"Thanks, Marv I owe you one."

"Never."

The next morning they left to go home. One day early.

CHAPTER TWENTY-EIGHT

Nick was keeping pace with the traffic.

"I spoke to Grossman; he says that he is going to try to keep you and Gerry out of the investigation. But, if it turns out to be a homicide, then it'll be in the hands of the Massachusetts State Police. More than likely, this is what it will be. As we were speaking, he told me that Clarice Vito was 5"9" and was a brunette with long hair."

Veronica looked perplexed.

"What's the matter?"

"The girl in my vision had red hair, and she didn't seem that tall."

"She could have changed her hair color but that doesn't explain the height difference. I trust you more than these reports, so this is something we'll have to watch."

❦ CHAPTER TWENTY-NINE ❧

"This is Dominic Ventura! Hello? This is Detective Ventura, anybody there?"

"Yes, yes I'm sorry, I dropped the receiver. I..." As Marvin Grossman brought the receiver to his ear, the cord caught on an open binder on his desk, dragging the phone base and all of the papers in front of it off the desk.

"*Shit, what's this opening night?*" He said to himself. Leaning over the side of his desk, with the cord stretched to its limit from the floor, he spoke into the mouthpiece. "This is Marvin Grossman from Long Island, remember me?"

"Hell yes, of course I do, the funniest detective alive. What's going on over there? And what's all that racket?",

He brought up the base and placed it back on his desk.

"I'm having some phone problems. My phone was down."

"Yeah that happens here too. An overload, maybe"

An overload, you got that right – me and the work.

"Every things okay now. What I called about is a missing person's case that I have and that you soon may be getting acquainted with."

"All right, let's hear it."

"I'll be brief. Two years ago two couples switched partners. Partner two was happy with partner one, but she is the one who is missing. Partner one male with partner two female, didn't work out. So partner one, the husband, became the prime suspect; however since then, partner two male has been arrested on a rape charge. You with me so far?"

"I'm on every word."

"We did the normal searches, phone records, computer hard drives; I don't have to tell you. He didn't tell us and we didn't find out about the uncle's house on the Cape. They took vacations there and get-a-way days. And they all knew where the key was kept; coming and going at different times. Now here is what I think we have. *I hope he doesn't hear me squirming.* I feel a search in and around the cottage, might reveal my missing person."

"You said cottage. How do you know it's a cottage as opposed to any other kind of dwelling?"

"I did say cottage, didn't I."

"Yes you did."

"All right, I'm going to be straight with you. One of my best friends, and a New York City detective, called and told me about his girlfriend's experience. It seems she dated the guy from couple number one and the guy from couple number two dated her friend. They were taken to the Cape and it's in that cottage that my friend's girlfriend got an eerie feeling that something went wrong there. She wasn't told anything other than that his wife is missing. This is all I know. Sorry I wasn't forthright with you, I was just trying to keep her out of it. By the way, we all graduated together from the same high school; the detective, his girl and her friend. They're not just acquaintances."

"Thanks Marvin, for being honest. More than likely we'll have to question both women, but don't worry; I'll do this deed or one of my associates, who is a woman. Is there one particularly eerie place that she felt might rank higher than any other?"

He doesn't think I'm telling him everything. But he's letting me get away with it for now.

"Yeah Dominic, try the river." He gave him the address of the cottage.

"Thanks, again, I'll be in touch."

Grossman put the receiver back on its cradle and began putting the papers strewn over his desk, back in order.

"Well that worked out well. It took me two seconds to give her up. Some *mench* I am." He said out loud.

❊ CHAPTER THIRTY ❊

They picked up little Nicky at the Labrador's house and brought him back to Nick's house. In the living room, Nick spoke first.

"Nicky, we have something very important to tell you."

Nick and Veronica were sitting on straight chairs and little Nicky was sitting on the floor between them.

"Roni and I are going to get married, and we want you to be happy about that."

He stood up and went to Veronica, and laid his head on her lap.

"I like you. Are you going to be my mommy?"

"I could never take the place of your real mommy, but yes, I want to be your mommy. I want very much to be your mommy."

She rubbed his head, while she spoke to him.

He left Veronica's lap and went to Nick.

"Thank you, daddy. I asked Santa Claus for a mommy and I always ask God, now I can ask for toys."

Nick hugged him and put his arm out for Veronica to join them.

❧ Chapter Thirty-One ❧

For the next three days, every one at work had seen her ring several times. They would ask to see it because it made Veronica beam and that, in turn, made them happy for her.

She was just back to her desk from her ring tour when the phone rang. It was her personal line.

"Gerry?" *Was she upset?* Is anything wrong?"

"I don't know, Roni. I just heard from Bill and he said his uncle from Florida, the one who owns the cottage, just called him and said that he gave the police consent to search the cottage. He said the police told him it has to do with Clarice, Bill's missing wife. He told them where the key is. Do you know he's 87? How did they find out about that place?"

"I...I told Nick about our trip to Cape Cod and he must have mentioned it to Marv Grossman, who's handling Bill's wife's disappearance. That's all I know about it. Maybe the cottage should have been part of the investigation? I'm sorry it upset his uncle but I guess they have to know about the places she might have been. Ken was the last one with her and everyone knows where the key is kept, even us. Bill shouldn't have to worry, but maybe Ken should. *Good, let me lay this on Ken.*

"You're probably right, Roni. It's just that Bill's so upset for his uncle."

"I've been trying to reach you and I've left messages on your answering machine. Didn't you get them?" Veronica asked.

"I haven't been home; I've been staying at Bill's. I'm still on sick leave."

"Well, I have some good news. Nick asked me to marry him. I have a ring, and besides Nick, I have a little boy to love. And I…well that's what's going on here."

She stopped, feeling that too much happiness might not be good for Gerry's feelings.

"That's really great, Roni. Congratulations! I have some news too. I was notified that Ken is out on bail. That's another reason why I'm staying here."

"Well, please tell Bill that it's normal to check out all places where his wife might have gone. I would love to see you."

"Roni, I'm sorry I'm in such a funk, its just that with Ken out walking around, it brings back a real bad time. I'll call you when I go back home or else I'll call you again from here. I know you don't want to call here."

"Thanks, I'll leave messages on your machine. Please stay in touch."

"Bye."

"Bye."

Veronica looked down at her ring and hoped that Gerry would someday experience the emotions that go along with a return of her love from someone like Nick.

❧ CHAPTER THIRTY-TWO ❧

Detective Dominic Ventura observed his team as they searched the cottage for physical evidence. The divers, provided by the fire department, would be arriving in the afternoon.

"Hey Boss, I don't think the bed in the front room was always in the spot that it's in now. It's been there a good while, but that's not its original place."

"Don't move it until you make the final sweep. Of course you know that."

In the department, Freddy was the shortest in height, but was held in the highest esteem for his experience. It was his thing to always call Ventura, *boss*.

"I see very slight indents over by the back corner. You want to come over here and look at this, boss?"

Ventura walked over to him, careful not to disturb the other work going on in the cottage. He got down on his knees and then put his face right at the floor, his nose almost touching it.

"How did you ever see these marks?"

"I'm short, remember?"

Ventura ignored the remark.

"And what about the bed, what did you see that made you think it wasn't always there?"

"That's easy, boss. See how the varnish is the same color and thickness under the bed as it is around the room. If that bed was sitting there for, who knows how long, twenty or thirty years, it wouldn't have worn that evenly."

Ventura was again on his knees, looking under the bed and still couldn't see how Freddy had come up with that conclusion.

The bed in the back room was a big, old, four-poster bed, which had to be taken apart to move and then be put back together again.

"This was never moved; it came with the house. Look at that floor? It was never walked on. And because of that, there won't be anything to scrape."

He was right.

Coffee was delivered and it signaled time for a break.

"This is a nice area, except for this house, which is probably worth over one mil anyway." Freddy said.

They all agreed with his view of the neighborhood.

Freddy turned toward Ventura, "We're pretty much done in the back room and finishing up in the front room. We have plenty of prints and what appears to be semen stains on both mattresses. The only thing left in the front room is to move the bed."

Ventura nodded approval at his thoroughness.

The team joined together in the back on the patio. There, coffee was embellished by a box of doughnuts, provided by Detective Ventura.

"I think the Cape is more about doughnuts than about tourists!" Freddy quipped.

They chuckled and agreed.

They put their coffee litter in a container, separate and away from the evidence bags.

∾

Freddy and the crew circled the second bed in the front room. All together, they lifted the bed in its entirety, frame and all. It was placed down in the back corner of the room; its original spot according to Freddy. There was a slight *ping* as they set it down. Freddy looked down at the bed, no one else seemed to have heard it. He jiggled the bed to see if he could hear it again.

The bed left a trail of dust balls that had to be gently swept aside.

Freddy called over to the crew sweeping the floor of the bed's former location. "I can see housekeeping was a lost art." He was still pushing down on the springs, trying to hear the *pinging* sound again and looking under the bed, to see if anything might have dropped off the frame.

One of the men sweeping the area called out, "We may have some blood here!" It was collected and put into its own evidence bag. This was their only blood sample.

Another shout came from outside the front of the cottage. "The divers are here from the fire department!"

Ventura went out front to meet them.

As they unpacked, Ventura reminded them about keeping the evidence intact.

"Before you start to bring anything up to the surface, check with me first."

The two man scuba team reported to Ventura and was given their instructions.

"I can't imagine anything lasting any amount of time in the middle of the river. Between the boats and the fishing lines, what we're looking for would have been snagged." He paused, "And what we're looking for is a body. So give most of your attention to the dock and to the base of the river closest to the cottage."

The team went into the river from the end of the dock.

Ventura went out onto the dock, and was looking down at the spot where the divers went in. He was bored with the house search and, based on Grossman's remark, he felt that this quest would yield better results.

After twenty minutes, one diver surfaced and pulled himself up onto the dock. He took his mask off.

"We got something!"

"FREDDY!

Freddy left his bed and came running out of the cottage.

"What's up, boss?"

"I want you to suit up and make sure things are done right. He tells me there's a bag down there, wedged in a cave-like place. He thinks he sees human remains. I don't know what the bag's made of, but I don't want it falling apart down there or up here. Take this full harness down with you and give it a pull when you have the package ready to bring to the surface. We'll start to haul it up. I don't want the harness to put stress on the bag, so on the way up, I want you and the firemen to support its bottom. Then, all of us, the crew inside the cottage and the firemen, will lift the entire package onto a gurney. We'll have our gurney as soon as I make the call to the ME's office."

Freddy got into his scuba gear and went down with the diver to the discovery. He saw the problem. *Probably easy for someone to get it down but gases and time have really wedged this thing in.* He tried to reach back and around it; there wasn't any room. He went back up to the surface.

It was Ventura's turn to ask about a problem. "What do we have, Freddy?"

"We're going to need digging tools. It's in pretty tight. I don't want to rupture it, so I think I'd like to loosen the lower boulder. It's right under our package and it doesn't look like it will cause an avalanche." He saw Ventura's pensive expression and added. "It's the only way boss."

They took down two long handled shovels from the basement and an edger that Freddy thought would be good for prying under the boulder. The pace was dictated by Freddy who orchestrated it as slow and steady. He had the edger and was creating a gap under the bottom boulder. Sand was cleared away as he went along until, suddenly, it moved downward and the bundle moved with it.

All three did the equivalent of jumping backward underwater. Freddy motioned them to stop. He moved in close and again tried to put his arm around back of the bag. He could, this time, until his gloved knuckles hit something hard and metallic. The bag budged, just a little. He motioned for them to start digging again. The boulder again moved downward, causing the bag to make a pronounced downward shift. Freddy raised his hand to halt their digging. He took from his belt the harness, being careful not to yank on it, causing Ventura to think it's ready to come up. The two firemen held it open as Freddy, this time, was able to get both arms around back. The bag slid out into the harness. Freddy went back to the now gaping hole and got himself half in before coming up against a metal container. He pushed himself out and yanked the cord.

On the surface, Ventura was cracking orders. As it broke the surface, the two firemen and Freddy lifted themselves onto the dock. At this point, the ME took over. The stench coming from the bag was overwhelming; how it was getting out concerned the medical examiner. One of the firemen was vomiting over the other side of the dock. The rest of the team, except for Freddy, were beginning to get green, and couldn't wait for the coroner to wrap things up and leave.

"You can get out of your wet suit, Freddy. Ventura motioned.

"Boss, there's something else down there."

"What is it?"

"I'm not sure. It looks like a metal box, footlocker type that has some rotted out sections. I pushed back in what I think was a human bone."

"Ask the firemen to hang here a little longer while I go tell the ME."

Freddy and the two firemen were in the water again. It was easier this time. The gaping hole provided enough leverage for them to break the natural binding the trunk had made to the rock. It was out and on the harness. Freddy checked the hole again to make sure this would be the last trip.

On the dock, they all stood around the locker wondering what, or who, was in the trunk. When the medical examiner returned, it, too, would join the bag at the lab in Sudbury.

Freddy had changed out of his wet suit and was back looking at the bed.

"Got a problem?" Ventura asked.

"Yeah, something, but I don't know what."

"I sent the rest of the men home. Let's move the bed back to where it was and call it a day and a half."

They lifted the bed and brought it back to its original site. When they let it down, there was that *pinging* sound again.

"Did you hear it?" Freddy asked.

"Hear what?"

"I'm calling it a pinging sound."

"No, I didn't. Ventura answered.

Frustrated, Freddy began lifting and bouncing the entire bed up and down. *Even if there is a ping, how am I going to hear it with this racket?* He stopped, with a final slam to the floor. A little gold ring dropped from the springs and rolled out from under the bed, landing at Freddy's feet.

"Well, what do we have here?"

Freddy picked it up with a tweezers and instinctively looked at its inside. The ring itself was tiny and the letters inside *C. O.* were almost too faint to see. Freddy saw them. He placed it into the evidence bag.

"It must have become caught in the frame; bounced in maybe? There's a "C O" on the inside. Maybe it stands for company and the rest is gone. What do you think boss?"

"I think it's a wrap. We did good today. The lab has a lot of work to do and I have a couple of phone calls to make tomorrow."

As Freddy logged in the final piece of evidence for the day, Ventura took a better look at the ring through the transparent bag.

"This is a significant finding," he said to Freddy. "Your persistence paid off big time. I'm guessing that this small ring has nothing to do with any wife disappearance and murder."

Ventura locked the front door and they stepped out into the balmy evening. He noted that crime tape had been used to secure what was now a crime scene.

❧ CHAPTER THIRTY-THREE ❧

"Hello?" Grossman called on Nick's private line.

"Hey Nicky! Marv Grossman, here!"

"Marv! How're you doing?"

"I don't know. I just got off the phone with my contact on the Cape, Detective Dominic Ventura, who's starting to wonder how I came about all this information. They fished out the body in the bag and, get this, there was another one right behind it, in a footlocker type of metal box. Their lab is examining it…all bones. He says it was there for a real long time."

"Don't stonewall anything on our part. If necessary, Veronica and I will meet with them.

"Thanks Nick, I'll keep that in mind. *Oh, you won't have any worries in that department, not with cave-right-in Grossman on the job.*

❧

Nick made a call to Veronica.

"Hi, Nicky! Veronica answered.

"I heard from Marv Grossman. They, the Massachusetts State Police, found not only the bag we found but another body in a metal footlocker. The second body, they say, was there a long time."

Veronica gasped.

"I think we should meet with a Detective Ventura. He's the homicide detective handling the case. There's something terribly wrong with that cottage, and it's not something new."

"Do you think I should let Gerry know?"

"No, not yet. Let the police do their job and when they're finished, I'm sure we'll be hearing from them; so will Bill and Ken. So far, I don't believe that Gerry is in any danger. When Bill and Ken are told, however, then I would like Gerry to act cautiously around them. We really don't know if they were involved. They could be completely innocent."

❧ CHAPTER THIRTY-FOUR ❧

Gerry showered before dressing for dinner. She looked at her naked reflection in the full mirror. *More toned than before? And perky breasts! Not working has its advantages.*

She put on a conservative dress, one of only two she had that went below the knee. Bill preferred this look, and Gerry didn't tell him that they were her funeral dresses. *I doubt that he was this particular with Roni.*

Gerry glanced at the mirror for the final once-over, and walked out of the soft carpeted guest room onto the hardwood floor of the hallway. She crossed the living room and stopped short of the den when she heard Bill, engaged in what she perceived to be a serious conversation. It was the urgency in his voice that caught her attention and made her stop. She hadn't heard the phone ring.

"I just don't like them snooping around." ...... After all these years, who knows?" ...... "Oh, and that one, you should know better then me." ......"No, no, no, I'm not accusing you of anything. I just meant that she was with *you* last, and not *me*."

Gerry felt uneasy eavesdropping at the doorway, and didn't want to get caught. She retraced her steps, this time, making noise on the hardwood floor before entering the room.

Bill looked away from the receiver at Gerry and then spoke into it, "We'll take up that problem tomorrow at the office. Gotta go, bye"

Gerry ignored the telephone call.

"Do you want me to cook dinner tonight? I make a great overdone steak and my undercooked pasta you could die for."

Bill smiled, "We'll go out."

ფ

In the morning, Gerry waited until Bill left for work before calling Veronica. While she had been staying with Bill, she insisted that she pay her way which would include using the telephone. For this call, she used her cell phone.

"Hi, Gerry, I was just thinking about you." Veronica answered.

"That lunch date, do you have time today? I'm still at Bill's but I'm thinking of going back to the Island tomorrow, to my place. I'm feeling much better."

ფ

They met and hugged each other outside of the coffee shop.

"You DO look good."

"I've been working out on Bill's equipment. His exercise equipment!" she quickly added.

"I didn't say anything." *That was almost the old Gerry, Veronica thought.*

They sat on opposite sides of a round wobbly table. Their coffee was served without saucers and each time they dipped into their salads, spillage had to be contained with napkins.

"I've had enough of this!" Veronica wadded a napkin, tilted the table and placed in under the short leg.

"That's what I've always admired in you...you don't let a table get the best of you."

Gerry's remark made them giggle for an instant.

"Roni, I don't know what or how to say this. But, before I do, I have to tell you that I'm so so happy for you."

"Thanks, and coming from my maid of honor makes it all the more special."

"Oh my god, oh my god, thank you, thank you." Gerry rose up over the table to reach out to Veronica.

They leaned over the table to embrace.

When they sat back, Gerry spoke first.

"Bill seems very nice and he certainly treats me great. The thing is that ever since his uncle's cottage became part of his wife's search, he's been different. Don't get me wrong, he still treats me better than anyone I've ever been with. It's just that I feel an undercurrent; maybe a nervousness on his part."

Veronica responded, "I think the move back to your own house is a good step. You've been through a lot and you're probably not as good as you think. A little break from men might do you good." *I'm not going to tell her what's going on on Cape Cod until I'm sure.*

"You're probably right. I went too fast, again, and now it's time for a time out." *Maybe I should tell her about that phone conversation. It's probably nothing,* Gerry thought.

Outside of the coffee house, Veronica called after Gerry.

"You be careful, and give me a ring when you get back to your place."

Gerry turned and nodded.

❧ CHAPTER THIRTY-FIVE ❧

"I understand, thanks, bye."

Ventura placed the receiver back on its cradle and spoke to Freddy.

"The ME's office said they're working on it. And, they said, without saying, don't bother us, let us do our job. Thanks to *your* tenacity, the best and only discovery, so far, is that ring. I found out from New York or, I should say, Long Island, that William Vito's wife's maiden name was Olson. Clarice Olson. It would fit the initials on the ring C. O.

Freddy shuffled his feet. "So what do we do next? We got everything out of the cottage and, I hope, we got everything out of the water."

He looked up at Ventura, who spoke.

"It's time I took a trip to the Big Apple. I definitely want to question William Vito and Kenneth Small and, to a lesser degree, Veronica Labrador and Geraldine McCabe."

"I'll get the paperwork ready, boss."

❧

Two days later, Ventura and a detective from the Mashpee Police left for Long Island and New York City. Before leaving, they received a positive ID on the body in the bag. It was Clarice Vito.

✖ CHAPTER THIRTY-SIX ✖

Veronica took the Long Island Railroad from New York early Saturday morning to be with Nick and Little Nicky over the weekend. He was waiting with Nicky at the station.

She greeted Little Nicky first, by picking him up off his feet. His soft face felt good against hers.

They each released their strangle holds and, with Little Nicky looking up at Veronica, she put him down next to the car.

"You give good squeezes."

"Thank you Nicky, you do, too."

Nick joined them with a kiss for Veronica.

At Nick's house, Little Nicky went off to the den to watch his shows.

"I didn't want to tell you over the phone that I spoke to Marv Grossman. There's a positive ID on the body in the bag. It's Clarice Vito. That's not a shocker. What is, is that the box behind the bag contained human skeletal remains."

"Oh my God! What's going on here? I saw Gerry yesterday; she's supposed to go back home today. I should call her."

"Hold on, hold on. If she's going back to her place, she should be safe there." I have more news; Bill posted the bond for Ken's bail. This I find very strange."

Veronica gave Nick a quizzical look.

"I find it strange, because I believe in my gut, that one of these guys is involved in what happened in that house. After what has turned up, why would either one of them be helping the other? They have to feel this way, too. It just doesn't make sense. And that's my job, making sense."

Veronica walked over to Nick's telephone. "I'm worried. I'm going to call my answering machine to see if Gerry left a message."

She dialed her number and code and listened. Her expression showed relief.

Nick placed his hand on her waist, "What's up?"

"She got back home and said that Bill was very good about it and would like to continue seeing her. She seemed happy, but she did say she's going to follow my suggestion about taking a break."

"That's great for Gerry. She deserves a break in her love life and Bill might not be the answer."

Sunday night, Nick took Veronica back to her condo in New York.

❧ CHAPTER THIRTY-SEVEN ❧

Bill answered his phone after the first ring.

"Hello? Oh. Hi Uncle Joe, how are you and Aunt Helen doing?"

"This is not a social call, Billy. What the hell do you have going on up there? The Massachusetts State Police just called and said there's a possible double homicide planted in my backyard. Do you know anything about that?"

"I know as much as you do at this point, Uncle Joe."

"The hell you do. They told me that one of the bodies was Clarice."

"I hadn't seen Clarice for six months before she disappeared. That's over two and a half years ago. She was seeing Ken during that time."

"Seeing Ken? How's that?"

"I was with Justine for a short time and he was with Clarice."

"For cripes sake, Billy, you're a lot smarter then that. That's just plain goddamn stupid."

Bill let him talk. He was his father's brother, the last one left from that generation.

"They told me that, for the time being, all they want is a statement from your aunt and me as to what we know. I told them we don't know donkey dust and that I've been down here over twenty years, but they want this statement anyway. Your aunt isn't feeling well and this news isn't helpful."

"I'm sorry to hear about Aunt Helen. But I swear to you, I'm as much in the dark as you. Clarice had gotten kind of wild there at the end and she did know about the key to the cottage. Ken says he didn't do it and I believe him. As far as the second body is concerned, it could have floated down from anywhere."

"Well, as soon as I settle in your aunt, I'm coming up. I should be up in about two weeks. You know you were always my favorite nephew. If I can be of any help…" His voice trailed off.

"Thanks, Uncle Joe. I don't think you should make an unnecessary trip right now. Let's see what the police come up with."

"Okay Billy, but you keep me up to date."

"I will, I will."

He purposely didn't tell him that he had been questioned by Detective Dominic Ventura earlier in the day.

∾

Ken Small was his next incoming call.

"A Detective Ventura is on the way here to question me," Ken said.

"And you'll tell him what you know. I believed you when you told me that you had nothing to do with whatever happened to her. And, as far as the other body is concerned, who knows?

"Billy!" Ken responded, but was cut short by Bill.

"I SAID, who knows? It could have drifted down from anywhere. The cops didn't give me any details."

"But I didn't have anything to do..."

Bill interrupted again, "But nothing Kenny, it's a fucking mystery. Let me know how it goes. Better yet, I'll call you."

"Okay," said Ken.

Bill Vito hung up the phone without a last response. His worried look couldn't be conveyed through the telephone. *He's beginning to make me nervous.*

❧ CHAPTER THIRTY-EIGHT ❧

Detective Eugene Boscarelli did the driving from Cape Cod and again to each appointment in New York. As he drove, Ventura went through his notes. Boscarelli was a new detective out of the Mashpee Police Department and, as was customary, a detective from the jurisdiction of the crime would accompany the homicide detective. He knew of Ventura's reputation from his friends at the Cape and Islands Detective Unit.

"So what do you think?" Boscarelli asked of Ventura.

"I think Vito and Small know more than we do and they're going to make us work hard to find that part out."

"As far as Geraldine McCabe goes, you just want to hug her for what she went through. I think her involvement with Bill Vito is trouble, but that's my opinion."

They were on their way to Veronica's apartment, where they had allowed Nick to be present at their questioning. Ventura let them have this liberty, since her connection was after the fact.

∾

Boscarelli circled the block several times until, to their luck, a space became available right in front of the condo.

They were passed through by the doorman and greeted at their doorway by Veronica and Nick, who introduced themselves and shook hands. Ventura and Boscarelli sat on upright chairs on one side of the coffee table and Veronica and Nick sat on a sofa opposite them, holding hands.

Boscarelli listened intently as Ventura asked the questions.

"Let me say at the start that this is not an inquisition. No one is accusing anyone of doing anything. I'm on a fact finding mission. We have two homicides, one of whom is a Clarice Vito. Since you have unknowingly been at or around a murder scene, I want to find out what you might have seen or heard."

Veronica shuddered and Nick squeezed her hand tighter.

"How long do you know Bill Vito?"

"About five months."

"Did you notice any quirks or did he ever perform any odd rituals."

"I didn't notice any quirks, as you say and, if he had any rituals, he didn't perform them with me."

"Did he ever show you any pornography or did you find any at his place?"

"No, and I never went to his place."

Ventura felt the glare coming from Nick even before he looked up from his notes.

"I'm very sorry Nick, I reluctantly agreed to you being here and…."

Veronica interrupted. It's okay Nick, you already know all of the answers, just let him ask his questions."

Nick sat back, still clutching Veronica's hand.

"Can I answer your next question without you asking it? I know where you're going and I'd rather not be asked this question."

Ventura nodded. "Please go right ahead."

"We didn't have intercourse or oral sex, but we were sexual. He didn't force himself on me and we didn't, nor did he ask me, to do some sexual aberration."

"That answer was as thorough as any question I might have asked." Turning to Nick, Ventura added, "Detective Vito has a gem and, as I understand it, this relationship began in high school?"

"Yes it did," answered Veronica. "And if I'm a gem, then Nick's my setting. Has a nice ring to it, doesn't it?"

Ventura and Boscarelli both smiled, but only Nick caught the double meaning.

Nick let go of her hand and put his arm around her. Her head instinctively went to his shoulder.

"I take it you came upon this information from Detective Grossman?" Nick asked.

"Yes, I did and he told me that he was also in the same high school class as you and Miss Labrador. I could sense the closeness; it's a nice thing to have when times are tough."

Ventura's cell phone, clipped to his waist, began to vibrate. The caller ID displayed his home phone number.

"Hello?"

"Maria, yes, I'm sorry. I moved the baby aspirin *bottle to the cabinet over the sink. Tell him I love him and that I'll be home tonight. Thank you."*

There was a pause.

"*Bye.*"

"Is someone sick?" Veronica asked.

"You understood? Do you speak Portuguese?"

"No, I don't. I guess there isn't a Portuguese word for *baby aspirin.* Veronica's eyes sparkled.

Ventura hadn't noticed them before and was momentarily mesmerized.

"Good catch! My youngest boy is only three and he's at home with a nanny. I have two girls in school and they'll be coming home soon. You see, my wife passed away last year and, like I said, it's nice to have good friends around you when you need them."

Now, why did I give out this information – was it those eyes?

"I'm sorry to hear that," said Veronica. Nick nodded in agreement.

"Thank you." Ventura shook his head in acceptance.

Ventura had closed his notebook while he answered his phone. He now opened it again. He looked over his notes concerning the cottage.

"Was there anything you noticed in the cottage, maybe an event that stands out?"

"Yes, I dropped my earring on the floor and it rolled under the bed and, when I fished around for it, I came up with a small gold ring."

Nick, who, again, was holding Veronica's hand, turned his head toward her and looked concerned.

Ventura's face couldn't hide his surprise, "You had the ring in your hand?"

"Yes, just for a moment. I dropped it and it bounced back under the bed."

Ventura closed his notebook. "You've been very helpful and I don't think we'll need to take this any further."

He shook hands with Nick, who had softened after being able to identify with him. Ventura and Boscarelli said their goodbyes to Veronica by taking hold of her slender hand.

Ventura got behind the wheel of their car. Boscarelli turned to look at the box in the back seat.

"Those swabs taken from Vito and Small will go the lab at Sudbury tomorrow," said Ventura.

"She is some knockout, and those eyes. Did you ever see anyone as beautiful?" Boscarelli asked.

"Yes, I did," nodded Ventura. *My Kristina,* he said to himself.

❧ Chapter Thirty-Nine ❧

"Coffee, Nicky?"

"Yeah, that'll be great. Did you see the look on Ventura's face when you mentioned the ring?"

Veronica turned her head away from the coffee maker and toward Nick, who was back on the couch. "What should I do?"

"I think it's more like what you have to do and when should you do it. I think you'll be visiting another evidence room; this time in Massachusetts."

"More people will know."

"I'll talk to Ventura about keeping this just between him and us. And, as I did, let it be chalked up to good old detective work. My hunch is that since both bodies were placed in the same location, the killer is one and the same or, if there is more than one murderer, they know each other."

"Bill and Ken," stated Veronica.

"Maybe," Nick shrugged.

"So, now what?"

"I'll call him in the morning and set it up."

❧ CHAPTER FORTY ❧

The phone rang in Ken Small's apartment.

"Ken? It's Billy."

"I know your voice," said Small. "I can't tell how it went but I know they don't like me. I just know they're going to pin Clarice's murder on me. The fact is, I didn't kill *anybody*. You *know* that. I fucked her, but I didn't kill her. And it was never rape. See, they got this charge on me, and I swear Billy, they're going to find a way to get me."

"I told you before that I believe you about Clarice. I don't know what happened to her. I think she went sex crazy after what we did. And who knows who she was with last."

"What about…?" Ken started to say, but was interrupted by Bill.

"Now you're making me nervous Kenny. That's another story, and I don't believe we have anything to worry about. Keep to your same routines; don't let this run your life. Remember CPA."

'What's that?" Ken asked.

"Can't Prove Anything!"

Ken gave a short, ha."

"In other words, keep it light. Still going to the gym? Still have your job?"

"Yes." Ken answered.

"Good, then all is not so bad. They'll find the murderer of Clarice, you'll plea out a lesser battery charge, especially with the lawyer you got, and everything will go back to normal."

"I hope so," said Ken.

"And another thing, Ken, don't call here for a while. I'll call you and we could meet some place for dinner."

After they hung up, Ken Small continued to look at his phone as if it contained additional assurance.

Bill made a call and left a message on Gerry's answering machine.

❦ CHAPTER FORTY-ONE ❦

Freddy stood in front of Dominic Ventura's desk.

"You're standing over me, why?"

"First of all, it's hard for me to stand over anybody. And, second of all, you left a message to come see you."

"You're right. I left that message yesterday."

"I had a personal yesterday." Freddy quickly responded.

"I'm sorry, Freddy. I think I'm losing it. With Tony being sick and this wacky case…. Anyway, I did call, and I do remember. I got a call yesterday from Detective Nick Vito who believes his girlfriend might be able to identify the ring you found. I have no idea what she could get out of that ring. What do you think?"

"I'm with you. It seems to be Clarice Vito's ring with her maiden name initials."

Ventura continued, "That ring holds more of a story then it's letting out. That's why I never mentioned it to either Bill Vito or Ken Small. I didn't want Bill Vito to tell me, yes, that's her ring when, maybe, she was never in there before they were married. He would then know we have a ring and he would be giving me nothing more than the obvious answer to my question. Kind of like asking a waiter, how's the food here?"

"Gotcha, boss."

"Veronica and Nick will be here tomorrow afternoon. Unless she has a good story, they won't be coming anywhere near that ring."

"Do you want me to hang around tomorrow?"

"I want you to be in the area, Freddy, in case I need you."

Freddy left the office with a semi-salute. Ventura returned the gesture.

∾

Ventura's anxiety was getting to him and he made a phone call to the Medical Examiner's office. He told them who he was and asked to speak to the ME himself.

"Ventura! I thought I said that I'd call you right before our report," said the ME shouting into his receiver.

"Sorry Al, there's nothing else happening here. The bad guys are getting stupider and stupider, pretty soon they won't need any more detectives." Ventura responded.

"Okay Ventura, only for you and off the record, it looks to be a young female, possibly a teenager. And, so far, that's all we have. Save yourself the phone calls and wait for us to do our thing."

"I hear you. I'll call you in a couple of days," said Ventura wryly.

❧ CHAPTER FORTY-TWO ❧

Veronica and Nick arrived at the Yarmouth Barracks at 2 P.M., and were greeted by Dominic Ventura and personally escorted to a private conference room.

"It's good to see you both again," Ventura politely began. I don't know what you could ascertain from the ring we found, but I'm sure you wouldn't have taken this trip for nothing. And, being accompanied by a detective who knows what I do, adds a certain mystery to this visit."

"What Veronica can possibly get from that ring, is more than you could ever imagine. She proved it to me by relating an incident which happened a long time ago. After telling me what she saw in the ring you have, she helped me with one of my cases. If she could be of help here, I'm asking you to keep her identity private. You will soon see why."

"I will tentatively agree to that request as long as what you say is true. You say she saw something in the ring. We thoroughly examined it, and all we could find were some ones initials. What could she possibly come up with?"

"I can see images!"

"What! Images? I expected something with a little substance, especially with you involved, Detective."

Ventura abruptly closed his note book.

"Now wait just a minute…" Nick started.

Veronica interrupted, "Detective Ventura, the ring you are wearing around your neck. Would I be able to hold it?"

"It was my wife's…" Ventura hesitated.

"I don't want to intrude but, in this case, I don't think she would mind."

Ventura slowly removed the chain with the ring on it from around his neck and took the ring off the chain. He had mixed feelings about having another women touch the ring, except that Veronica implied a certain faith. He placed it in her open hand.

The only outward sign was a body spasm. Within her mind, the images were revealed to her. She turned her hand over and let out the ring on the table.

Ventura's eyes went from the tabled ring to meet the soft stare of Veronica. A tear trickled down from the corner of her right eye.

"She is very beautiful and the nurses did up her hair the way you liked it. You told her that you loved her, and always will, forever. And…" Veronica stopped and shook her head.

Ventura took the ring and Veronica placed her hand over his. With his lips quivering, he said, "Thank you. We can go over to the evidence room now."

∾

It was deja vu as she entered the room; a carbon copy of the one back in New York. She stood, as before, at a shelf. Ventura left them there.

"Are you okay? Nick inquired.

"I'm fine, Nick. I had no idea…I…It was impulsive. If I'd known, I wouldn't have done it."

"It was a good idea, Roni…a good idea."

Ventura returned with a ring in a clear plastic sleeve. He took it out of its container and placed it on the shelf in front of Veronica. He nodded at her to take it.

The girl was naked and was laughing and pointing to something. There were two others. She was pushed down on a bed and was now being choked.

Her knees buckled as she tried to put the ring back on the shelf.

"My God, she was choked to death on the same bed that I was in." Veronica felt it coming and couldn't stop it. Her knees buckled, again.

"Nicky, Nicky…"

Nick sensed it too. He caught her and put his hand on her forehead, as she vomited in the corner of the room.

∾

Ventura had Nick wait with him in his office for Veronica to return from the rest room.

"Cop to cop," Nick said. "I'm asking you to please keep this, and anything involving Veronica, just between us."

"Cop to cop, request granted." Ventura quickly replied.

"You've got some girl there." Ventura added.

"I know."

Veronica entered the office.

"I'm so, so sorry. Emotions play a huge part with my stomach, always have. But I'm sure that my stomach is not what you want to talk about."

"Take your time. Take as much time as you want," said Ventura.

"Could I have a glass of water?" Veronica asked.

"FREDDY!" Ventura called out.

Freddy poked his head in the door and did a double take at Veronica.

"Could we have a glass of water for the lady? In fact, make that three glasses, please."

"Would you want a slice of lemon in them, Boss? Just kidding, coming right up."

"Freddy's been with me a long time. I gave up a while ago trying not to have him call me boss. He's a good man."

Veronica took a sip of her cold water.

"You have a cooler?"

"Yes we do," replied Ventura.

"She was small," Veronica began, "almost child like, maybe a teenager. She had long red hair, a small nose, maybe freckles. There were two others, males. Again, young, maybe they were teenagers too. I couldn't make them out, but I could tell that the bed was in a different location, from the time when I was there at the cottage. The girl was laughing and pointing at one of them, and then she was pushed down hard on the bed. I think it was the one she was laughing at, that had his hand around her throat. There was some mention about a river. It went dark after that." Veronica shuttered.

Ventura looked at Nick and then at Veronica.

Veronica took the cue. "I think I could use a little fresh air."

"FREDDY!

Freddy poked his head into the office.

"Could you please show Miss Labrador around our establishment? You can skip the downstairs den of detectives."

"Gotcha, boss!"

"The missing person's report on Clarice Vito told us that she had long dark hair. And at 5'9" she would be taller than the description given by Veronica. She was probably that height as a teenager, given the female growth cycle. This makes the ring belong to the second body." Nick stated.

"That's how I see it, Nick. Can I call you Nick?"

"Sure, boss." Nick smiled and so did Ventura. "Yes you can, and for you, Dominic, Dom?

"Dom is good," answered Ventura.

❧ CHAPTER FORTY-THREE ❧

They were both quiet on the way back to New York from Cape Cod.

Veronica spoke first. "I don't ever want to do this again."

"You won't have to. I promise you, I will never ask again and I won't let any one ask you either. I spoke to Ventura; you will be kept out of this. You're officially out of the ring business."

They were almost through Connecticut.

"Nicky, I'm not trying to play detective but has Justine Small ever been questioned about her time with Bill."

"I read Grossman's report, it was pretty thorough. Nothing was spared and Justine was very candid. Do you have something in mind?"

I'm not sure. There's something about Bill that's different in an odd way." *How can I discuss Bill's problem in bed. I can't, not with Nick.*

"Odd in what way?" Nick asked, without turning his eyes from the road.

"He likes darkness instead of light. Maybe Gerry has taken this further and there's something to it. Or, maybe she didn't experience this at all and there's nothing to it."

He didn't want to ask her in what way Bill liked it dark. "Okay, I'll check with Gerry. Remember, as they say, little things mean a lot."

You don't know how on the money you are Nick, Veronica thought.

❦ CHAPTER FORTY-FOUR ❦

On the sidewalk outside of The Rathskeller, they reached out for each other with extended arms.

"This is nice," Gerry said.

"For me, too," replied Veronica.

At 5 P.M., The Rathskeller was already alive with a growing population. They took a table off to the side and away from the snowballing crowd.

"Hey, you look great," said a smiling Veronica.

"And you, you're beaming like the bride you're going to be. Nick has had a positive affect on you. I'm so happy for the both of you."

They ordered their drinks and their dinners at the same time.

"I'm sorry I dragged you into this Bill-Ken fiasco. It didn't exactly work out the way I thought it would for me. And for you…," Veronica's voice trailed off as she placed her hand over Gerry's.

"I'm all right now. That's a done deal and don't blame yourself for *my* poor choices. I went with Ken and then I went with Bill. I wish there was an immune system for self image." Gerry smiled.

Veronica laughed out loud, loud enough to cut through the noisy din and turn heads away from their conversations. Some of the heads stayed turned.

"Now that's the old Gerry, one who I've missed terribly."

There was a pause while they sipped their wine.

Gerry looked up from her food. "The old Gerry received a call from Bill yesterday. He left a message on my machine to call him. He was nice and all that and, while I was with him, he wasn't aggressive. I needed to have that, but after a while, I wanted to feel normal again, normal and whole, without having to lean on any one."

I'm glad you brought Bill up and not me, Veronica thought.

"Did you notice anything different, *there*, about Bill?" Veronica asked using her eyes.

"*There*?" You mean, *there*?"

"Yes Gerry, that's what I mean," Veronica said with a giggle.

"You've really come a long way. Well, the night before I went back home, and while we were watching television, I began to feel normal again, normal and horny. We were sitting next to each other on his couch. I had on a long night shirt, nothing special. We kissed, and when I went to straddle him, he said let's go into my bedroom. We had separate bedrooms, in case you wanted to know. The bedroom was dark, even though, earlier, I thought I had seen a light on."

Gerry leaned over the table and spoke in almost a whisper. "He was finished before I could even get ready for him.

I tried to help, but his hand blocked my way. The funny thing about this is, I think he thinks, we had sex. I left the next day."

Veronica chose not to relate her experience and Gerry didn't prod. They finished their meal and made a pathway to the door and out onto the sidewalk.

"I know you didn't ask and I thank you for that." Gerry said. "I don't plan on seeing Bill again. He's not what he appears to be and maybe worse. Thanks for being my best friend; I couldn't be happier for you and Nick. Oh…and little Nick, he sounds adorable."

"We'll do this again, soon," said Veronica.

They hugged and then waved as their parting gesture.

Gerry turned and called back, "That Detective Ventura can interview me anytime!"

Veronica laughed and waved back again.

∾

On Friday night, Veronica went out from the City to stay with Nick and little Nicky.

"Coffee is ready and we have the last of the frozen Cape Cod bagels. I can't believe, as New Yorkers, we're freezing bagels from Cape Cod. But you know what? They're the best!"

After little Nicky gave an ecstatic greeting to Veronica, he went off to watch his shows.

"I had dinner with Gerry this week."

"How is she doing?"

"She's doing great and volunteered a few things concerning Bill. And, to sum it up, she said she believes that Bill is *inadequate*. In other words, he has a *small* problem.

Nick's brow furrowed questioning her statement.

"Okay Nicky, there are several ways to say this, but to put it bluntly and still be classy, Gerry believes he is not well endowed; he has a small penis. Maybe that's what the young girl in my vision was laughing at, not knowing how much you guys worship size. I didn't *see* who was in the house with her but I bet that's what it was."

"I'm going to make you an honorary detective, *my* honorary detective. This is Ventura's case. What I'll do is recommend him questioning Justine Small. She was forthcoming the first time with Grossman and, hopefully she'll be the same this time. Ventura could lead Justine into revealing more of his *little* problem and then have the ammunition needed to lean heavily on Bill. And Gerry can be kept out of it."

❧ CHAPTER FORTY-FIVE ❧

It was an easy pick-up; almost as if she sought *him* out. Ken liked that idea. It was 9 P.M. and he was sitting at the bar in Frank's Bistro and Lounge when she brushed against leg, going between his stool and the empty one to his right. He turned to look at her profile. She was staring straight ahead, as if trying to get the attention of the bartender.

Ken took the initiative and called out for her. "Hey, Barry, the lady needs a drink."

She turned toward him. "Why thank you."

She was very attractive, about fifty. Her long blond hair went well with her slim figure, he noted.

"Hi my name is Ken."

"Hi back, my name is Gail."

She crossed her legs and the slit in her fashionable below the knee length skirt revealed most of her thigh. Ken took it all in and she knew it.

Since being out on bail, his job routine on Fridays was to take his car into Manhattan. This way he could stay as late as he wanted and avoid taking the subway back up to The Bronx. Next Friday, he had plans to meet Bill after work, spend the evening in the City and then he would take Bill home to Queens. It would be like old times.

He bought Gail that first drink and then the next two. Their stools had gravitated closer and she had placed her arm around him. His hand was on her thigh as they talked, nursing the third drink.

"Do you have a car? She asked.

"It just so happens I have. I live up in The Bronx, but I drive in each Friday."

"My home is on Long Island. Maybe you could take me to the station. I know a place where we could stop before that, though."

Ken Small couldn't believe his luck. They went together to the parking garage and, with Gail's directions, they drove to a secluded area by the docks. He was rough with her and she let him be. She undid his belt and brought his pants down to his ankles. Her bra was off and he reached up her skirt.

"I'm sorry Ken; I'm going have to pee. I'll be right back."

She straightened her skirt, buttoned her blouse and got out of the car.

Gail turned back and spoke through the open passenger side window. "Please hold the moment!" She pointed to the side of the building they were parked next to. "I'll be right back," she said again.

It was at this point that he noticed her white formal gloves, which she hadn't worn in the bar.

She turned at the corner of the building and kept going.

Ken caught the flash in the side view mirror.

"Huh?" He said in recognition.

The knife came down and hard into his neck. He tried to raise his arms, but it was too late. His head flopped to one side. The huge knife was pulled out and wrapped in a towel. Ken was pushed over the console and a gloved hand took his wallet from his sport jacket pocket.

✣ CHAPTER FORTY-SIX ✣

It was 6 A.M. Saturday when Nick received a call at home, *a possible homicide down by the docks.* He left Veronica and Nicky at his house and drove into Manhattan. He was met at the scene by Mike McLaughlin. "The car is registered to a Kenneth Small, Bronx address. He didn't have any ID on him."

"I know him! He's been charged with rape here, and possibly a double homicide in Massachusetts. Or, I should say, he was.

Nick examined the wound.

"A huge blade did this. Looks like a double edge. Pants at his ankles might mean he had a passenger. I don't need to tell you to go over the entire car."

McLaughlin understood that it was procedure for Nick to tell him and not that Nick thought he would be remiss.

Back at his desk, Nick made a call to Dominic Ventura.

"They found Ken Small this morning, dead in his car; stabbed through the neck. As soon as I have any more on this, I'll let you know right away."

"Thanks, Nick. In this business I shouldn't be surprised and, yet, I'm surprised every day and this is no exception."

"I think this makes us partners of a crime," said Nick

"Nice play on words, keep me informed, partner." Ventura responded.

"I will, and you stay safe."

On Monday morning, Mike McLaughlin was waiting for him to arrive.

"Get this Nick. When the coroner removed Small's body from his car, they found a white bra under him. Size 32C!" The remark didn't get a response from Nick and McLaughlin didn't expect it would. "Another thing, there were no finger prints other than Small's on the passenger side or in the entire car for that matter."

"This is starting to look like an assassination, made to look like a robbery; pants at ankles, no prints, possible missing prostitute," said Nick. He continued, "Calls have come in since yesterday placing him the night before at Frank's Bistro. A "Barry," the bartender, was supposed to have seen him there. I have an idea. Get me a picture of Bill Vito; you can get it from the Department of Motor Vehicles."

∾

Nick called ahead to Frank's Bistro and found out that Barry would be working the lunch crowd. He walked in and motioned Barry to the side of the bar. He showed him his ID.

"I'm Detective Vito."

Barry extended his hand and said, "Barry Clarke."

"Barry, I understand that you knew Kenneth Small and that you were working the night he was killed. The women that was with Ken Small, that night, did you ever see her before?"

"No, Detective, I never saw her here before"

Barry was muscular and wore a shirt that emphasized his upper body build. He was polite and Nick could see that he was seriously thinking back to that night.

"Could you describe her to me?"

"She was old. You know, maybe forty?"

Nick smiled and didn't let him continue.

"Barry, look, I know you're a young guy…how old are you?"

"Twenty-six"

"Twenty-six," Nick repeated. As he gazed around the room for a good example, a familiar face came through the entrance.

"Gerry!" He called out.

Geraldine McCabe came running over to him. She looked svelte, in an off one shoulder white top and a flirty and flippy rose print miniskirt.

"I heard it on TV and read it in the news," she said while hugging him. "It was a horrible way to die, even though he was a horrible person."

"So what brings you here?" Nick asked.

"They have the best brisket of beef in New York." She looked over at a group of women standing at the entrance. "I'm here with some people from my new job. I work in the City now; my job is great and I'm looking to move into the City like Roni. I saw Roni the other day, I'm just so happy for the two of you, actually for the three of you."

"Thanks, and thanks for including Nicky. Do you know Barry?"

"Of course I do."

She gave him a wave and he nodded back.

"I've dominated enough of your time," said Nick. "Go join your friends; hopefully we'll see each other soon, maybe over a barbeque."

"I would like that."

They kissed and she turned back toward the entrance.

"What do you think of her?" Nick asked Barry.

"She's awesome, man."

"She's forty-one, Barry.

"No fucking way! Oops, I'm sorry."

"That's all right, now let me ask you again, how old do you think the women with Ken Small was?"

"Let me think…, taking everything into perspective, if Gerry looks as good as any thirty year old or less, than the women with Ken Small looked forty, but could have been fifty."

This kid isn't stupid.

"Now, that's what I'm looking for!" He gave a thumbs-up to a beaming Barry.

"I have another request; I want you to look at this picture."

He showed him a picture of Bill Vito.

Barry starred at the picture trying to stay helpful to Nick.

"I don't know him…, but…hey, I did see him here about a week ago and he was with the woman you're asking about. I *did* see her before."

"Good. Tomorrow morning I want you to call this number. I'll give you the directions and you can come to my office and we'll see if you can identify the woman from some pictures of ladies we have on file."

❧ CHAPTER FORTY-SEVEN ❧

Tuesday, on Long Island, was a designated school holiday because they had used only one snow day during the year. Nick made an appointment to speak to Ken Small's ex-wife.

Justine Small fit her married name. She was petite, not more than 5'2" with above the shoulder blonde hair and a bang constantly falling down across her forehead. Justine answered the door of her modest Cape Cod style house dressed in size two jeans and a white *world peace* tee shirt.

She extended her hand to him. "Hi, I'm Justine Carson." She saw the look on Nick's face.

"I've gone back to my maiden name. Actually, I never changed it with the school so that was the easy part. I remained Miss Carson."

She brushed the bang back, again, and Nick wondered how many times during the day she did this and if it was distracting to her class. They sat at her kitchen table.

"First off, I want to thank you for giving me time on an off day and..., well, I'm sorry again for whatever loss you feel."

"When you offered your condolences over the phone, I thought, what for? But after I said thank you, I thought about it. We lived with each other for over seven years, and there *were* some good times. There were also some weird times, as you well know. He never harmed me, though, and I never felt afraid."

She paused. "The fact that we switched partners, will that get out? It didn't when Clarice disappeared. Maybe it didn't as a favor to me because my father was a captain with the Nassau County Police."

She neatly dropped that, Nick thought. *I see Grossman's hand in this.*

"I don't see where that is relevant to Ken's murder but, if it was, I couldn't suppress that kind of information; not in a murder case."

Justine nodded her head in understanding. She swiped at her lock again.

"I only have a couple of questions. "Do you think your ex-husband would be capable of murder? I know you're thinking, he was murdered, what kind of a question is this? Please just give me your gut reaction."

"I would have to say no. He never hit me, he never even pushed me. I know he was accused of rape and beating some one. I know he's a suspect in poor Clarice's disappearance and then murder. I just can't relate him to any of this."

"When was the last time you went up to the cottage on Cape Cod?" Nick asked.

"About three years ago, Ken and I both had some free time and went there in the winter. This was before we switched spouses, which was the dumbest thing I ever did. Bill Vito had egged Ken on, who didn't need much prodding when it came to sex. While at the cottage, I remember Ken had to fix a window to stop the snow from coming in. We had a good time, he was nice then.

"It was Bill's idea to switch partners?"

"Yes."

"What went wrong with you and Bill Vito?"

"In a word – sex. He wasn't good at it. I think he was trying to find a person who would not be disappointed."

Nick didn't take it any further. He knew what she was saying and she knew that he knew.

"Thank you, Justine, you've been very helpful. I will try not to have any of your painful details become public."

"Thanks, Detective Vito, and I'm happy to know that you're not a relative of Bill Vito."

Nick shook her hand and smiled.

❧ CHAPTER FORTY-EIGHT ❧

On Tuesday evening, Nick met with Bill Vito at his home in Queens, New York. Bill's house was in the middle of a tree lined block. They were attached *row houses* that had a garage, which ran underneath on the right side of a stoop; steps that rose up to the front door. As Nick took the top step, he saw Bill looking through the screen door. Bill swung the door open out, causing Nick to step back. *A little show of one-up-manship,* Nick thought.

He extended his hand to Nick, who briefly shook it and then let go. Turning his back, he *led* Nick into the dining area.

"Please take a seat," said Bill.

He looked like someone holding a winning hand as he tried to knock Nick off his game, "We share the same last name. Maybe there are family ties back in Italy?"

"Maybe," Nick said. *But I hope to hell not!*

With the same "cat that swallowed the mouse" look; Bill noted again, "Are you on this case because of Veronica?"

Nick controlled his emotions. "No, it's a normal assignment," he said tersely. *This guy is some piece of work.*

Nick continued, "I offer my condolences for the loss of your wife and the loss of your friend, Ken Small. Detective Ventura has briefed me on the two murders that took place at your uncle's cottage on Cape Cod. Of course, one of those was your wife Clarice." Nick's tone turned authoritative. "I'm not here for that. I'm here to find out what you know about Ken Small's last days." As Nick spoke, he stared into Bill's eyes without wavering, causing Bill to blink.

"I... read about it in the paper this morning...we grew up together. He's my oldest friend, or was. I still can't take it in."

Nick had all he could do to keep a straight face at such bad acting.

What a crock of shit. Should I run and get a cold cloth for your forehead?

"Yes, I know what a difficult time this is for you, but I have to ask some questions; seeing that you were best friends and all of that."

"No, no please go ahead; I know you have to do your job."

"I understand you have quite a gun collection. Does that Bowie knife on the wall mean that you might have a knife collection also?" Nick asked and pointed.

The knife was hung in a case, over the mantel of a gas fireplace. The case had a glass face which was etched and it's mahogany case had brass hinges.

"It's a replica!" He was off his chair and the case was opened before Nick could tell him not to bother.

"See, it's dull."

"Do you have any others like this with a double blade?"
Maybe he'll get jittery if he knows what we're looking for.

"Well I…I didn't buy any knives other than this one. I always admired Jim Bowie and wanted his knife." He handed the knife to Nick, who didn't take it.

"It's all right; I don't want to smudge it." *Maybe he got a little jittery?*

Bill Vito placed the knife back into its case and, while his back was turned, Nick looked past the dining area and into the adjoining den. The large screened television dominated the room, but around it and in the surrounding entertainment unit, was an unusual amount of audio equipment. Bill saw Nick taking interest in his den and he began fumbling with the key to lock the knife case. Nick took this opportunity to walk into the den area, pretending to be interested in the television set. Bill didn't follow him.

"This is a nice set. I just went for a plasma one, myself. The next time you upgrade, you should consider it; they don't take up much space."

"I'll do that."

Nick sensed that Bill was uncomfortable with him in this room.

"You have quite a collection of audio devices. Let's see, besides the usual, you have mikes and a…gee, reel to reel. Haven't seen that lately. How do you use all this stuff?"

"I originally recorded practically the entire history of rock and roll onto cassette tapes. Now I'm transferring them over to disks."

That's a short answer to a lot of equipment.

Nick walked back to the dining room and pretended to look at his notes.

"Ken was found around the corner from two gay bars. Do you find this significant? Do you know any reasons why we should pursue this area of investigation?"

"Like I said, I've known him since we were kids. He never showed any signs of being a little light in the sneakers. If anything, he was just the opposite."

"You mean gay, don't you?" Nick said in an acid tone.

"Oh eh, yeah, I eh…, right, gay. But I can't say he wasn't eh…, gay. He raped Gerry and I didn't think he was capable of that either."

He's feeding him to the lions, some friend.

"Well, you've been very helpful and if I have any other questions I'm sure you will be as cooperative again." Nick glared at him looking for a quick response.

"You can count on it." Bill was quick to answer.

Nick, *this time*, walked to the door with *Bill in tow*. He swung open the screen door and turned to accept Bill's outstretched hand. Nick gave his same tepid shake with a quick release. As he went down the stairs, he could feel Bill Vito's eyes drilling him from behind. *Fuck you!* Nick thought.

CHAPTER FORTY-NINE

Nick returned to his office in time to hear his direct phone line ringing.

"Nick, here!"

"Nick, this is Dominic Ventura."

"Hey, how are you, Dom? You were going to be my next call."

"I'm fine. I have two pieces of info that should be of interest to you. First off, missing persons, here and in Ireland, believe that the body belonged to that of a, Claire O'Flaherty. It would match the initials in the ring and would coincide with the time of her disappearance. She was a temp worker who worked at an ice cream store in Hyannis, since closed. Both here and the authorities in Ireland believe that it's her. I doubt that forensic could do any better. However, her family provided us with baby teeth and we will be following up our conclusions with DNA proof."

"That's good work. And it does give her family closure and provide a burial place to mourn. What's the second piece of news? Can you tell me who the murderer or murderers are?" Nick said in a voice not expecting a yes answer.

"Yes, I can!"

"What?" Nick exclaimed.

"The ME found a hair on a folded over piece of duct tape that was in with the body of Clarice Vito. The DNA matches that of Ken Small and unless you can tell me anything to the contrary, I'm going to close this case. What do you have?"

Nick paused.

"Dom, what I have is the extreme dislike of Bill Vito and, maybe, I want him to be guilty. That's not good law enforcement. He's not behaving like he's innocent, which is not helping my slanted view. And, I have him linked to the murder of his buddy, Ken. My gut feeling, and as you know, it's a big factor in our business, is that Bill has a dark side. Ken is bad but I believe Bill is sinister. I don't have to tell you it takes a certain type to commit a murder, especially of a woman or a young girl. Bill fits that mold…Ken-I don't know."

"I see what you're saying. Tell you what, I won't close this up just yet. I'll let the lab continue to run its tests."

"Thanks, Dom. It won't be much longer on my end. You'll hear from me as soon as I get something definite."

Nick shuffled some papers on his desk and a small card with Justine Small's name and unlisted telephone number on it surfaced. He made a call.

∾

"Hello Justine, this is Detective Vito, again. I'm sorry to bother you but I have one more question to ask you."

"That's all right; I'm here grading the worst test scores I've ever seen. Just when I thought I was making some headway with this class. Anyway, ask your question, I could use the break."

"Remember when you told me that you had a getaway with Ken at the cottage on the Cape and that while you were there he had to fix the windows?"

"Yes."

"Could you tell me what Ken used to fix the windows?"

"Sure, it was a roll of duct tape he found in a closet."

"Now think carefully, you know how duct tape, after you use it, disappears into the roll and the next time you need it, you have to dig it out. By any chance do you remember if Ken did something so that wouldn't happen?"

"I don't have to think about that one at all; we did live together. He always folded over a piece of the tape and then cut that off the next time he used it. He was a fanatic about that and, if I was using it, he would remind me more than once to fold over the end."

"Thanks, Justine, you've been very helpful. Test scores aside, you have a great evening."

The call ended with goodbyes and, again, a request from Justine to help keep her private life private. Nick, again, assured her he would try to honor her request. With the receiver back on its cradle, Nick slammed his open hand on his desk.

"YES!"

❧ Chapter Fifty ❧

On Wednesday at 10 A.M., Barry, the bartender, was passed through security at Manhattan North. He was through his second book when pizza was delivered. Mike McLaughlin was taking care of feeding him the books and getting lunch. Barry was using McLaughlin's desk, where an area was cleared for the books and now expanded for the pizza.

"This is the best this desk has looked in a while." McLaughlin noted.

"How many books do you have?" Barry asked.

"You have one more to go from the active generation and then we'll start on the semi-retired to just retired." Mike answered. "We have many more volumes downstairs in the archives; more pictures than your entire stock of beer bottles in the *Bistro*. It's a popular profession and runs the gamut of socioeconomic groups."

Mike McLaughlin was proud that he had earned a degree in Criminal Justice from Pace University this past year, and wanted to *sound* like he had graduated from college. He didn't mind that he had earned the label of *super cop*, he wanted to let everyone know that he had also earned a college degree.

Barry washed his four slices of pizza down with a coke without stopping his quest and without getting red sauce on the books. He looked at his watch, it was 1:30 P.M. He was due at Frank's Bistro at 5PM. Barry factored in a shower, change of clothes and travel time – he needed to get out of here by 2:30. He opened the third book.

"They're starting to all look alike"

Barry stared down at the first picture on the page.

"That's her!" He pointed. "Younger in this picture, but that's her all right."

McLaughlin looked over his shoulder.

"Gail Perkins…I remember her; real smart, took her in myself, maybe ten years ago. She shouldn't even be in that book. Let me see…"

He went to his computer scrolled through a list of names.

"There she is, Gail Perkins, a.k.a. Dale Smith, a.k.a. Gail Conroy. Says here she's gone legit or as legitimate as she could be until we catch her. You've been a great help, Barry. Here's a get-out-of-jail card for when you need it. They shook hands.

"Thanks, and say hello to Detective Vito for me."

"Will do," said Mike.

∾

Gail Perkin's unlisted telephone number was breached and an appointment was made with her for Thursday morning. She was noticeably caught off guard, since only her clients had access to her number.

"Detective who? Vito? When were you thinking of needing me? I'm booked until…you want to what?"

"We need to ask you some questions concerning an incident that you might have some knowledge of. You can either come here or we can come to you. It'll be very informal."

She didn't need to ponder. She had been *there* and didn't want any old memories to be stirred up or meet any old friends. *Better my house than their house.*

"You can come here."

"Tomorrow morning?" Nick asked.

"Fine," she said.

✖ CHAPTER FIFTY-ONE ✖

Nick wanted a partner to go with him to her apartment and when he found out that McLaughlin had arrested her years ago, he seemed like the perfect candidate.

"You can come with me and reacquaint yourself with an old friend," Nick told him.

On Thursday morning, at 9 A.M., they drove over to the East Side on Lexington Avenue and found a space (not a parking space) at the corner of her street. They parked with their wheels up on the sidewalk. Mike McLaughlin was driving and put up a placard on the dashboard.

"I don't know why people find it so tough to park in this city," noted Mike.

Nick gave him a wry smile.

"Nice...place. Business must be good," Mike observed.

Nick turned to Mike and said, "You keep looking, I'll be handling all of the talking from this point on."

Mike got the message and nodded.

The doorman stepped forward and Nick showed him his badge.

"Official business," Nick said.

"Yessir," he practically saluted.

"She even has a doorman," said Mike.

Nick turned around to McLaughlin and said, "Looking, taking notes and giving me your undivided attention, all done quietly."

"You'll have no trouble from me," said Mike.

"I hope so."

As Nick started to knock, the door suddenly opened. Barry was right, she was a fifty year old that could pass for forty or younger. She had long blonde hair and her face was wrinkle free. She was wearing gym shorts and a tank top. Nick showed her his ID and did his introductions. Mike said nothing and followed them into her living area.

Nick spoke first. "Gail, let me say before we get started, that your picture was recognized from a certain book we have on file. It was recognized by an employee of Frank's Bistro as the person who left there with a man named Ken Small."

"I don't know any Ken Small."

"Well that may be, but he was murdered that night. And under him we found a white bra. What was the size of that bra, Mike?"

Since being told to sit still, Mike had all but checked out on her soft tan couch. What he was checking out were the high ceilings. At 6'5" he appreciated the expanse above his head. He snapped to.

"The bra, yes, it was a size 32C." Mike caught himself looking at her breasts and then looked away.

"Now Gail, we can run a DNA test on this bra, or you could save us the trouble if you could remember if you lost your bra that night," said Nick

"Oh my god…I didn't know, I didn't know. I know what you're thinking, but I'm not in that line of business anymore."

"Well what line of business are you in Ms. Perkins, the last time we met, I was taking you in for just the type of pickup you did with Mr. Small. Remember me? I'm Detective McLaughlin, now."

Mike McLaughlin looked over at Nick, who nodded his approval.

She did remember a rather tall cop taking her in, but didn't acknowledge it, or him. She looked at Nick.

"I have an escort service. I file a schedule C on my income tax return and pay all of my taxes. I'm not in that line of work anymore." Gail stated in a steady voice.

"And what about poor Mr. Ken Small, where does he fit in?"

"I was hired by a "Carl" and was told to pick up Mr. Small, go with him in his car and then go over to this spot on the West Side and 29th Street. Just before we were to have sex, I was to find an excuse to get out of the car. Supposedly pictures were being taken to be used in a divorce. I swear to you, that's all I know."

"Who set this up with you?" Nick asked.

"It was this person named Carl. We did everything over the phone, including Small's description. I never met Carl."

"Is this Carl?" Nick showed her a picture of Bill Vito.

"No, that's Bill. I go out with him sometimes."

"So how do you know that Bill and Carl aren't one and the same person?"

"I told you, I go out with Bill. I know his voice and they were very different."

"How different?" asked Nick.

"Carl's voice was lower and gravelly."

"I'm going to give you the benefit of the doubt, that you don't read newspapers or listen to the radio or watch television. You know you are obligated to come forward if you know, or certainly if you can figure out that you might be the last person to see a murder victim. News was light that night and this murder was all over the media. I want you to be honest with me. I don't want to be dragging information out of you."

"She looked at Nick and said, "I understand."

Nick gestured with both hands, palms out and raised his eyebrows; a signal for additional information.

"This "Carl" paid me in cash, in an envelope passed through from the doorman. After that night, I didn't have any further contact with him. I do have something else though; when he called, he left a message on my answering machine. It wasn't erased, I still have it. There is a problem; I have a lot of other messages on my answering machine which is part of my phone. It could be an embarrassment for some people."

"Erase all the messages except for "Carl" and give me the phone. Do you have a back up answering machine?"

"Yes, it's an old cassette model. I have two other phones, so that's not a problem."

She erased all the other messages, disconnected the wires and handed Nick the phone. "I just got this, it handles four lines. Plus, it has lots of other bells and whistles."

"I'm going to take care of this myself and I'll have this back to you as quickly as I can," said Nick.

Gail turned and opened a drawer from the cabinet where her phone once stood, and brought out her old answering machine. Wires were wrapped around the unit and McLaughlin helped her set it up, with a telephone brought in from another room.

Downstairs, Nick approached the doorman and showed him the picture of Bill Vito. "Are you the doorman that took an envelope for Ms. Perkins and is this

the man that gave it to you?"

"Yes sir, I took the envelope up to her, but this doesn't look like the guy who gave it to me."

"What did he look like?" asked Nick.

"Well that's the thing, his nose was bandaged, like he broke it, and he had on a big baseball hat."

"What do you mean by big?"

"It covered his whole head, up to his ears. It was strange looking but, at the time, I thought it had to do with his injury."

"At the time?"

"Yes, now I think it was just strange."

As they drove back, Nick protectively cradled the phone.

"I'm going to bring this to the tech unit. I'm sure that as soon as their voice print analyzer goes to work, we'll have Bill's voice and we can pick him up and end all of this.

"I would like to have listened to all of the messages," said McLaughlin.

"She's cooperating Mike; no need to make this case any bigger by going off on a tangent. Her business is her business and her clients business is theirs. If we have to dig to find a crime being committed, then the world is a far better place than what's depicted, every day, on page three of the Daily News. After I return this phone, I'm going to forget her address. You should, too."

❧ CHAPTER FIFTY-TWO ❧

The tech lab extracted the message off of the phone's answering machine and, responding to his request, Nick received a call to pick up Gail's telephone. He was told that it was definitely a voice synthesizer and their voice print analyzer would interpret the voice and remove the synthesizer effect; giving them a true voice print. He thought back to all of the audio equipment in Bill Vito's house.

It was 4PM on Thursday. He made a call to Gail Perkins.

"I have your phone and could drop it off tomorrow morning."

"That would be fine and fits into my schedule," Gail responded.

Her schedule... this is a heck of a job, he thought.

Nick called it a day, early, and looked forward to the weekend, when he could spend time with Veronica.

∾

On Friday morning at 9 A.M., Nick was again on Gail Perkins's street and parked in the same space as before, tires on the sidewalk. He tucked the telephone under his arm and proceeded up the city block. Nick tried to call before he left but her phone would only ring and ring. He wondered why the answering machine didn't pick up. *Maybe it wasn't hooked up right, or it was too old to work, in any case, if she isn't there, I'll leave it with the doorman.*

The doorman was the same one he spoke to yesterday.

"Could you tell me if Ms. Perkins left her apartment this morning?"

"I haven't seen her, sir, not even for her early walk, and I didn't see any visitors for her this morning. Her last visitor was last night at 11:30.

"Is that unusual for her to have a visitor that late?"

"Yessir, she doesn't get much in the way of visitors."

Nick decided not to give the phone to the doorman. *Her phone keeps ringing, late night visitor, no morning stroll and last, but not least, the guy with the broken nose.* Something's wrong.

Nick went up to the apartment and knocked on the door. He didn't wait too long for a response before taking out his handkerchief and trying the door handle. It wasn't locked.

The atmosphere at the entrance didn't give Nick much confidence. He called out her name and took two more steps into the apartment, where stillness ruled. As he walked down her carpeted hallway, he instinctively drew his 9mm Glock, holstered at his waist. He went past what he believed to be the guest bedroom and toward a light coming from a door at the end of the hall. This would be Gail's bedroom. *It's always the bedroom.* He no longer was calling out to her.

Nick pushed open the already ajar door, bracing himself for what he had seen dozens of times. The room was empty; the bed was still made. Nothing in the room seemed to be disturbed. He had been lead to this room by its light and the fact that it was the bedroom. Nick went back down the hallway to the part of the apartment that he was familiar with.

Gail Perkins was lying face up on her soft tan couch, her head on a green pillow, on the couch's arm. There was another pillow under her ankles. Her arms were outstretched over her head and tied at the wrist; secured to a leg of the couch. Her legs were fully extended and her ankles were tied and secured the same way. She was naked.

Were those pillows there to make her comfortable before you choked her to death?

There was a rope burn around her neck. He didn't want to disturb anything until the experts did their thing. Nick bent down on one knee to take a closer look at her neck. Her head was to one side and on the back of her neck he noticed a pinch mark. *If she was choked during an act of passion, like this whole scene is supposed to represent, then how come the rope or whatever he used, has the point of closure behind her head? She was choked from behind and then "set-up" on the couch.* He scrutinized the room, which looked no different than it was yesterday, when he was here with Mike. He remembered the telephone. Nick went over to the phone area and instinctively took out his handkerchief. He didn't need it. The hatch was flipped open on the old answering machine and the cassette was missing. Her appointment book lay open next to the phone with a page on the left side ending with last Monday and the page on the right side beginning with next Monday. A page was missing.

❧ CHAPTER FIFTY-THREE ❧

Nick got back to Midtown North after securing the crime scene at Gail Perkins' apartment. He called in Mike McLaughlin.

While McLaughlin stood by his desk, Nick made a call to the apartment management company and, after getting a telephone number, he made a call to the night doorman.

"The doorman told me that her visitor had a bandage over his nose and a big hat. And get this, the doorman spoke to Gail Perkins over the intercom and she said it was all right for this guy to go up. I want you to pick up Bill Vito. I want him off the street. By the time you bring him in, I'll have proof that he's committed a murder or two or three."

As Mike turned to leave, Nick's telephone rang.

"Hold it, Mike!

"Dom, how are you!"

"I'm fine and I have some good new for you, Nick. Our lab has come up with another piece of duct tape and this time it has another hair follicle, possibly ripped off from a finger. And they tell me that the chance would be one in a million not to be Bill Vito. I'll fax you the request to pick him up."

"No need. We're in the process of doing that right now."

Nick pointed to the door and Mike understood. He raised his right hand to Nick, as he left in a hurry.

"I think he's gone over the edge, Dom. I got him involved in two murders down here and, who knows, he probably did that poor little Irish girl many years ago. I'll keep you on board."

Nick got in touch with the Crime Scene Search Unit and was told they agreed with him, that Gail was strangled from behind. They added that her clothes appeared to have been taken off after she was dead and that the only prints other then the victim, belonged to Mike McLaughlin, taken off the answering machine.

∾

His phone rang again. The lab had completed the voice print analysis and, to save time, Nick asked that they play it for him over the phone. It was Bill Vito explaining how they were going to exchange cash for services. Nick could feel the momentum driving this case forward and the fact that Bill Vito's "wheels were coming off."

He called Veronica.

"I won't be able to meet you until late tonight. I'm sorry."

"That's okay; I was going to call you. I promised Gerry that I'd stay with her. We're going to do some Long Island things, like shopping malls, and then you could pick me up in the morning. You don't happen to know any single cops do you?"

"No...well yes...I, look Roni, this is not a good time."

"What's wrong?"

"We have a warrant out for Bill Vito. Don't be alarmed, but I do want you to be extra careful. I spoke to Ventura from Cape Cod and we're all but certain that Bill was the one who killed his wife. He's also a prime suspect in two other murders, and he was probably the one who killed that little girl many years ago. He's becoming unraveled, Roni. Don't take any chances and pass this along to Gerry. Maybe it's a good idea to stay home with Gerry."

"Oh my God! Oh my God! Please be careful Nicky. He's not worth it. And don't worry about me and Gerry, we're tough chicks. And besides that, he's not interested in us anymore."

"Don't take it lightly, he's a killer who uses different weapons *and* he has a gun collection."

"All right Nick, we'll stay home in her house tonight.

Nick took one of the unmarked cars, threw his maps, notebook and cell phone on the passenger seat and drove toward Queens and Bill Vito's house.

❦ CHAPTER FIFTY-FOUR ❦

Gerry's phone rang and rang until her answering machine intervened. After Gerry's message, Veronica spoke.

"Hi Gerry, I'm on the Long Island Expressway and should be to you in about twenty minutes. Are you out picking up goodies or are you...?"

"Hello, Roni," Gerry answered the phone.

"Are you screening your calls? You know, you can use your caller ID. It does the same thing without being so obvious."

"This isn't a good time for you to come over. Something came over me, maybe a twenty-four hour virus."

"Is there something wrong, you don't sound right?"

"No, definitely not, you know how I get when I feel sick, all spooky and stuff and I begin to think that I'm sicker than I really am."

"Spoo...?" She caught herself. "Oh, all right, I'll call you tomorrow to see how you're feeling."

She's never used "spooky," ever.

She didn't know why, but Veronica's sixth sense told her not to say anything about Bill

"What did you mean by *spooky*?" Bill asked.

An hour ago, Bill had arrived at her door, "just wanting to talk." She had looked out of her window and didn't see his car, which was parked around the corner. Before driving to her house, he checked with her job and was told she had taken a vacation day. Calling ahead to see if she was home, he used his blocked phone number. She answered her phone and he hung up. Her caller ID displayed "unidentified number."

Gerry opened the front door, but not the screen door. They spoke with the screen between them.

"I...I just came to talk." Bill stammered. "I feel so bad about whatever happened between us. I...I would like to see you again. You're a decent human being Gerry and I know I've made mistakes, but if we could start slow and see how things go..."

Gerry's finger was on the screen door latch. Bill heard a slight movement of the latch; she was checking to see if it was locked. At the sound of her securing her safety, he shoved the door open, breaking the flimsy locking device.

She belonged to him now.

"What did you mean by *spooky*?" Bill asked again.

"Oh, that's just how I always expressed my over statement of any ailment that I might have. Roni and I said I got spooked and turned whatever I had into something worse. Like a headache into a brain tumor or heart burn into a heart attack. That kind of stuff."

Gerry could feel the sweat running down under her arms. She had on sweat pants and a light pullover.

"I don't believe you. I think that was a signal to your good, frigid friend. When she shows up, she can join our party. And, I hope she tells her fucking boyfriend or whatever he is. By signaling her, you did exactly what I wanted; I wanted them here. He ruined it between me and her and he's going to pay for that. I got nothing to lose."

"Are you going to kill me?"

"No, but if you don't do as I say in my little party, I will." He said this as he waved a 9mm Walther P99 back and forth.

❧ CHAPTER FIFTY-FIVE ❧

Nick's cell phone had been left in the vibration mode. When Veronica called, he was nearing the entrance of the Mid-Town Tunnel and in the midst of a traffic jam and a horn blowing contest. Nick smiled at the futile ruckus while Veronica was leaving a message on his phone. Traffic let up and he drove into the tunnel.

∾

Veronica continued her trip to Syosset.

Something was wrong with Gerry. If she's sick, then I could help; why then did she say spooky? Maybe it's nothing and maybe it's Bill. If that's the case, I'll wait for Nick.

∾

Dusk had given way to night. Most of the houses on the block had their outside lights lit and other light coming from fully exposed windows or creeping through drapes and shades. All except Bill's. His was a dark mass. At the top of the garage door was a row of small windows. Nick went back to his car and rummaged around in the glove compartment, flipped the trunk lock and looked in. *I can't believe it, no flashlight.* He went back to the glove compartment and then noticed the door pocket. He found a small flashlight in the passenger side door.

Nick climbed the front stairs which rose above and to the left of the garage. With his left hand on the upper stair guardrail, he leaned over to the right and shined the light into one of the small windows. The garage was empty, meaning Bill was on the move.

When he returned to his car, he picked up his map to move it out of his way and noticed the cell phone message light flashing. He saw the number belonged to Roni.

Nick listened as she told him about Gerry trying to cancel tonight and then Gerry using a possible code word, *spooky.* This was Veronica's favorite word.

It all adds up to Bill, Nick thought. He tried to call her back and received a message that he had reached her voice box. He remembered that Gerry's house was in a dead zone. Nick left Roni a message not to go into Gerry's house and that he was on the way.

❧ Chapter Fifty-Six ❧

It was dusk when Veronica arrived at Gerry's house. Her house was alive with light and the only car in the driveway or around the house belonged to Gerry. Veronica parked in front and walked up the cement path to the front door. She looked around again and into the house. Everything seemed normal, including sounds coming from Gerry's kitchen television.

Veronica's hand went to the screen door and it was then that she noticed that it was bent at the door handle and that the locking mechanism was torn off. Before she could fully realize the danger, the front door swung open revealing Gerry with an arm around her neck and a gun pointed to her head.

"Come in Veronica, I've been waiting for you," Bill said.

"Bill, why are you doing this? You're just going to get yourself into a whole lot of trouble."

"Take a seat, Veronica, or Roni, or whatever pet name Nicky boy calls you."

Gerry and Veronica were physically led to a couch in the living room which was visible from the front window. Bill stayed off to the side, out of sight from the street, with his *Walther* pointed at them. They held hands.

"I'm sorry," Gerry said softly.

"It's not any one's fault, we met them together, remember?" Veronica whispered back.

"How touching, it's all because of me, the big bad wolf. I was good enough until he showed up!"

"Why are you doing…this?" Veronica asked again, her voice catching.

"Oh, now is the beauty going to cry? It's you! Don't you understand? He took you away…he came back and took you from me. I really loved you."

"You need help," said Veronica in a steady voice. "This is only going to get worse, don't you see?"

Gerry joined in, "Please let us go and we'll say you didn't harm us, which could go well for you." She turned to Veronica, who nodded her head in agreement.

"It's too late for that." He looked at Veronica, "You pushed me into this, I have no way out of this quicksand, except to get my revenge. It they don't already know, it won't be long before they find out that I've killed other people."

He didn't say who but the key word here is "other." Veronica thought.

"Even if that's so, wouldn't it be better to end it here and give yourself up. If you didn't harm us…" Veronica was interrupted.

"I guess you don't understand. I didn't come here to let you go. I came here to get revenge on Nick. It wasn't exactly the way I planned it." He pointed at Gerry. "I was going to hold you hostage for a while." He then pointed at Veronica, "And have you come over followed by your boyfriend; just the four of us, nice and cozy with no other cops."

Veronica and Gerry became quiet and squeezed each others hand.

The shoulder bag, which was ripped from Veronica's grasp, was lying at Bill's feet." He bent down and, with one hand, rummaged around the main compartment.

"Let me see, did he provide you with protection?" His hand went around the cell phone.

"Well what do you know, you have a missed call from, oh let's see, it says it's from Nicky, isn't that sweet. Give me your password or she's (pointing at Gerry) going to need plastic surgery. Remember, I got nothing to lose."

Veronica gave him her password.

"He's on his way *Ron...ee*," he said in a mimicking tone. "Your hero is coming to rescue you. I couldn't have planned it any better."

❧ CHAPTER FIFTY-SEVEN ❧

Nick had been to Gerry's house many times before because she had lived here with her parents during high school. Still, he slowed to a crawl as he made a left turn onto her street. At mid-turn, his headlights were directed at a white Toyota. It was Bill's car. Nick was momentarily startled at his discovery and stopped; then moved quickly past. He pulled his car in front of Bill's and parked bumper to bumper. Nick picked up his cell phone.

"Hello, Mike? Instead of Mike McLaughlin, the phone answered back with a mechanical voice that the party was unavailable. He left Gerry's Syosset address.

Seconds later, Nick's phone vibrated with an in-coming call.

"Nick, don't go in, wait!"

"It's Roni, Mike. I don't have a choice. Call the Nassau cops for backup." Nick closed the connection and turned off his phone.

Nick walked down the tree lined street on the opposite side from Gerry's house. Every home on the block was a split level, a staple of Syosset. He stopped and stood behind a tree just across from the house. The front window was fully exposed and he could make out two figures seated together facing the window.

It was Roni and Gerry sitting together and looking out at the street. Looking for what? Me? This is a set-up. They're not looking at anything, some one's watching them!

Nick crossed the street and went around the back of the house next to Gerry's. He kept the two cars in the neighbor's driveway between him and the neighbor's view. Once in the backyard, he jumped over a chain link fence into Gerry's yard. The back sliding door leading to the downstairs den was open and the sliding screen wasn't locked. Nick slid the screen and it made a grating noise; he immediately stopped. He looked through the screen and into the dimly lit den, listening for any indication that he might have been discovered.

Tearing it wouldn't do any good, too many crossbeams on the door.

He decided to take the slider out of it's frame. He had a small pen knife on his key chain which he used to raise the sliding bottoms wheels on the door up and over its track. As he did the second set of wheels, Nick held onto the cross beams so that the door wouldn't fall back into the house. He swung the door in, placed it on an angle and lifted it out onto the brick patio. *Did they hear me?* He stood motionless in the den, listening for any activity from the floor above. There was none. *Did I hear a television set, before?*

Nick removed the 9mm Glock from it's holster and went to the carpeted stairs leading up to the main floor. He gingerly ascended, expecting at each step to encounter a loose board. When he had neared the top without a sound, he felt compelled not to take any more chances and took the final two steps at the same time, putting him in the kitchen area at the back of the house.

Where could Bill be?

There was a hallway leading to the front door, with the living room and dining area on either side.

I can't go down this hallway; he's probably on the other side of this wall, watching them.

To avoid the hallway, Nick went through the open area from the kitchen into the dining room. At the front of the room, he could look past the front door into the living room. He saw Veronica and Gerry, sitting as before.

Somewhere outside of the house was a noise and, at once, the house became a discotheque. Three police cruisers had arrived unannounced, lights flashing. Bill revealed himself from behind Veronica and Gerry to see what was happening on the street.

Nick didn't see a weapon. "It's over Bill! Step away from them!"

Inside the house, it sounded like a sonic boom. Simultaneously, Nick felt his stomach burning. He was falling forward, loosening his grip on his weapon and now had met the floor. Veronica was at his side.

"NO! NO! NO! NICKY!"

She knelt down and her left hand went to the wound at his middle. Veronica's jeans were already soaked at the knees with Nick's blood. Her right hand was on his leg; he was trying to tell her something with his eyes. She understood.

Bill was ranting and laughing.

"Now what do you think of your big hero? Look at him; he's drowning in his own blood!"

In one motion, Veronica slid her right hand down Nick's pant leg to his ankle holster and removed his snub nose .38 as she had seen *him* do many times while securing it. Her first bullet, using one hand, put a perplexed look on Bill's face. He pointed his Walther at her but not before she had added her other hand to the .38 and pulled off the remaining four rounds.

Sirens were wailing outside. Gerry had made a call for the ambulance and now was letting in Nassau's finest. Emergency medical technicians rushed through the door and Veronica let go of Nick's hand and was sobbing. She heard them call ahead about a gun shot wound. She listened as they used the words,…shock…hemorrhaging…it was all becoming a blur.

Gerry helped Veronica to her feet. "We'll follow them, Roni. They're taking him to the Medical Center (Nassau University Medical Center). They said it's better equipped than Syosset. Roni, please bring it together, *please*."

"I…I need to call my father."

"Here's my cell," said Gerry.

"Daddy, you have to do me a favor. Drive over to Nick's house and pick up little Nicky from the sitter next door and bring him to your house." She tried not to, but made a guttural sob into the phone.

"What's the matter Roni, what's happened?"

"It…it's Nick, he…he's hurt badly. I can't talk, Daddy, please just take care of Nicky until I get there."

Gerry couldn't keep up with the ambulance and fell behind. She wanted to say something to Veronica but couldn't find the words. Tears rolled down Gerry's cheeks as she bit her lip to keep herself from crying. She could not have drowned out the stifled sound of a broken heart.

❧ CHAPTER FIFTY-EIGHT ❧

Veronica came through the doors of the emergency room of the Medical Center with Gerry, one step behind and was greeted with a bear hug by Mike McLaughlin. Beyond his big frame, she saw a sea of blue uniforms. Mike looked at the blood on Veronica's blouse and jeans, bent over on her shoulder and broke down.

"He's in the Emergency Center," said Mike into her shoulder.

McLaughlin let her go as a nurse guided her to a small room, away from the main area.

Veronica turned to Gerry, "Could you wait here for me?"

"Sure… yes, of course, Roni."

Within ten minutes, a doctor opened the door to Veronica who had remained standing

"Hello, I'm Doctor Jacobs. Ms. Labrador?" he asked as he held out his hand.

"Yes, I'm Veronica Labrador," she noted.

He sat down on a white padded bench in the room that had two other white stack chairs, separated by a matching table with magazines on them. Jacobs motioned for Veronica to sit next to him. "Please sit," he said.

She wanted to ask how he was, but her instincts told her this was what Doctor Jacobs was here for.

"I understand that Mr. Vito is your fiancé?"

"Yes."

"There's no easy way to say this, Veronica," he started. "I must be truthful; he's lost an awful lot of blood, too much blood, among other damages. Nicholas' pancreas and several arteries have been compromised."

"What does that mean?"

He paused and took a deep breath. He has less than a fifty, fifty chance. I'm so very sorry.

She put her head on Jacob's shoulder and wept.

"He…he has a little boy. I mean *we* have a little boy."

"Is there some one you want to call?"

Veronica didn't answer him.

"Can I see him? Can I be with him? Veronica asked.

"Yes, of course, you may stay with him as long as you want."

"Thank you."

Jacobs escorted her to the doorway, but didn't follow her in.

She tried not to look at all of the tubes and monitors and whether they were all attached to Nick. To her, they were a bad omen. *I don't want to know what they do because they can't help him get better.* She slid a small aluminum chair as close to the bed on his left side as possible.

"Nicky," she said softly. "It's bad, Nicky, it's bad."

His eyes, which were looking straight up, turned toward her.

"I love you, I love you," she said. Tears rolled down her cheeks and around her chin. She looked at his face, as if for the first time, and broke it down into parts. *His nose was so perfect, like from a Roman statue. Those soft brown eyes, that spoke what his heart felt. Did I ever notice his ears and how they fit his face so well?* She moved her face closer to his, trying to join with his and go wherever he might go.

He startled her by speaking in a slow but steady tone.

"I can do this Roni, because I can feel your love and I'll have it forever. My heart is full, not of sadness, but of this love." Nick paused to gather more strength.

Veronica kissed him. "I will take care of Nicky for the rest of my life. I will try to be the best Mommy possible. He will know how good his father is and that he is a hero and that he has the best Daddy in the world and that…" She stopped. "Oh Nicky, how can I do this?" she sobbed.

A tear appeared at the corner of his left eye and slowly trickled down to his ear.

"You can do it, Roni. You can do it, I know you can." There was a break, as he took several deep breaths. I'm feeling a little drowsy, maybe it's the drugs. I love you. I love you." *Please let these be my last words.*

"I love you Roni, I always have…I love you."

Nick's eyes fluttered, but before they closed, Roni spoke, "I love you Nicky, I always will."

Nicholas Vito passed away at 1 A. M. that morning with Veronica at his side.

When Veronica stepped out of the room, Gerry was there to hug her.

"I…" Gerry tried to speak.

"I know," Veronica said in a steady voice. "I need your help with a few things."

"Anything," said Gerry.

"I'm going to ask you to take me to my house, and then to Nick's to get some clothes for little Nicky."

At her condo, Veronica changed her clothes and packed some more into a suit case. She did the same at Nick's house for little Nicky. Gerry, instead of being a caretaker, stood back and admired Veronica's resolve.

❧ Chapter Fifty-Nine ❧

Gerry's house looked gloomy. "I can never live there again," said Gerry. "I'm going to my aunt's house tonight, but I know I can never live there again."

"You can stay at my place in the City if you want. I'll be staying at my parents with Nicky until I can sort out our lives."

"Thank you, thank you. I'll take you up on that. I loved you both so much. I feel that my heart has been twisted around and that a piece of it has been lost forever. I can only imagine how you feel." Gerry lowered her head as she sobbed uncontrollably."

"I need people around me to remain strong to help me."

"I understand and I'm going to try and be that person for you, Roni."

Gerry wiped her eyes with her outstretched fingers.

Veronica picked up her car parked at Gerry's house and drove to her parents. Gerry took her car and drove to her aunt's house in Hicksville.

During the short ride, Veronica felt her chest in the area where she believed her heart was and it hurt to the touch. *Is this what a broken heart feels like?* She parked her car in their driveway. Her father was waiting at the door.

"Is Nicky sleeping?"

"Yes, honey, he is."

"He's gone, Daddy."

He held out his arms and held her close. "I know. It's been on television. They didn't mention his name but I knew it was Nick that they were talking about. Mommy put Nicky to bed in your room and she's been in our bedroom ever since."

"I just need to lie down; probably not sleep, just lay down." Veronica said.

She went to her old room and found Nicky asleep in her bed. She stood at the doorway looking in and at how peaceful Nicky was as her father went to her parent's bedroom and closed their door. Through the closed door, she could hear both parents crying, probably in each others arms. She had never heard Charles Labrador cry before.

In the morning, Veronica called Gerry on her cell phone and asked if she could accompany her to make the funeral arrangements later that day. As she hung up the phone, Charles Labrador put his hand on her shoulder. "Do you want me…"

"No daddy, this is what I have to do, what Nick expected me to do. I'm his mother."

Nicky finished his breakfast and was going to watch one of his shows. Veronica took his hand and brought him into her bedroom.

"Nicky," she said. "You know that I love you."

He nodded.

"Last night something happened to your daddy. You know that he's a very brave policeman, a detective."

Nicky nodded again.

Please God, give me the strength.

"There was an accident and your daddy is not coming home. He went to meet your mommy in heaven. He didn't want to go, but he had to because he is so brave."

Veronica put her arms around him, not knowing what reaction he might have.

He looked into her face, "When will he be coming back to see me?"

"That's just it, he's going to have to stay with your mommy and I'm going to be your new mommy. "I love you so much."

"My daddy is not coming back to see me?"

Veronica squeezed him as they both cried.

"It's okay to cry, Nicky," she said through her tears, and held him away from her for a moment, so that *he* could see *her* grief. She resumed holding him tighter than before; for both their sakes. His arms were wrapped around her neck with their cheeks touching and their tears uniting them.

Veronica delayed the wake and funeral for two days and stayed at Nicky's side.

❦ Chapter Sixty ❦

TWO YEARS LATER

Veronica's private office phone rang. She had just gotten off that line with Gerry. Aside from her parents, no one else, of late, had been given this number.

"Hello, this is Veronica Labrador."

"Hello, Veronica, this is Dominic Ventura, Detective Ventura, remember?"

She had last seen him at the wake and he had also attended the funeral.

"Yes, of course I do. How are you?"

"I'm fine thanks. And how are you and Nicky, and little Susan, is it?"

He had stayed in contact with Marv Grossman, who kept him updated. When Suzanne Vito was born, Ventura sent Veronica a congratulatory card.

"She's Suzanne, everyone makes that mistake."

"I won't again," Ventura slipped in.

"They're both great, thanks. Nicky's doing real good and having a sister, I think, has helped him. He's her servant, and enjoying every minute."

"That sounds so good Veronica, I'm really happy for you."

"I know phones are deceiving Dominic, but you *do* sound close, and is that a New York subway I hear in the background?"

"Very good! Yes it is. I'm in New York on business and wondered if you had some time available and would like to join me for a cup of coffee? Do you?"

"Yes," she answered, almost involuntarily. "Yes, I would like that."

Full lyrics of song:

Our Time of Love

When I hear your name I can see your face,
I can feel my heart aching inside.
As the years go by I can't stop that feeling,
of wanting you by my side.

Life for me is not complete and though I pray,
I can't erase the reason that pushed you away.

I'm sorry for the pain that I caused you,
and I wish I could tell you that I still care.
You will always be in my heart,
and this is my hurt to bear.

(Refrain - Repeat 2X)
It should have been our time of joy
It should have been our time forever
It was our time of love

(Ending)
And now I can only wish that we'll meet again someday
That life will give me another chance and take this pain
away.

❧ ABOUT THE AUTHOR ❧

TOM SALVADOR was born in The Bronx and formerly of Long Island, New York. He now resides with his family in Cape Cod, Massachusetts.

Printed in the United States
45894LVS00001B/16-24